THE VANDERBEEKERS
of 141st STREET

By Karina Yan Glaser

CLARION BOOKS
An Imprint of HarperCollinsPublishers
Boston   New York

For Dan

Clarion Books is an imprint of HarperCollins Publishers

The Vanderbeekers of 141st Street
Text and interior illustrations © 2017 by Karina Yan Glaser
Map copyright © 2017 by Jennifer Thermes

www.harpercollinschildrens.com

The Library of Congress has cataloged the hardcover edition as follows:
Names: Glaser, Karina Yan, author.
Title: The Vanderbeekers of 141st Street / by Karina Yan Glaser.
Description: Boston ; New York : Houghton Mifflin Harcourt, [2017] |
Summary: Told that they will have to move out of their Harlem brownstone just after Christmas, the five Vanderbeeker children, ages four to twelve, decide to change their reclusive landlord's mind.
Identifiers: LCCN 2016031664
Subjects: | CYAC: Family life—New York (State)—Harlem—Fiction. | Landlord and tenant—Fiction. | Neighbors—Fiction. | African Americans—Fiction. | Harlem (New York, N.Y.)—Fiction.
Classification: LCC PZ7.1.G5847 Van 2017 | DDC [Fic]—dc23
LC record available at https://lccn.loc.gov/2016031664

The text was set in Stempel Garamond.

ISBN: 978-0-544-87639-2 hardcover
ISBN: 978-1-328-49921-9 paperback

Printed in the United States of America
23 24 25 26 27 LBC 20 19 18 17 16

"Home was the coziest, pleasantest place in the world."
— Elizabeth Enright, *Spiderweb for Two*

"Home and I are such good friends."
— L. M. Montgomery, *Anne of Green Gables*

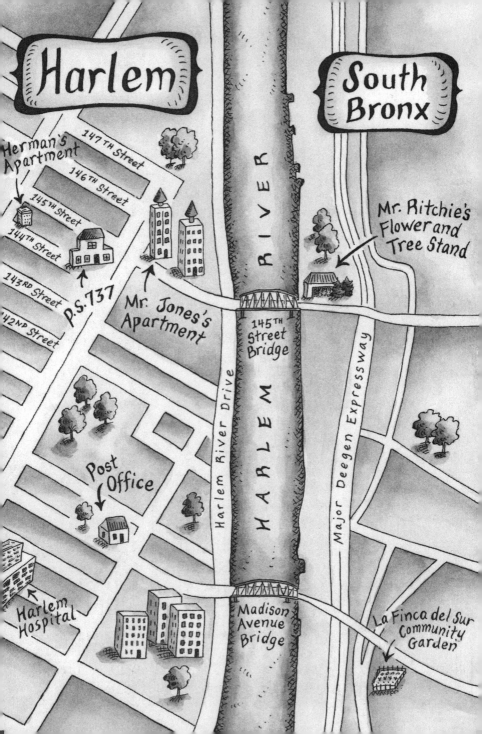

FRIDAY, DECEMBER 20

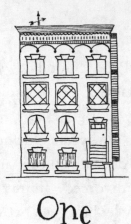

One

In the middle of a quiet block on 141st Street, inside a brownstone made of deep red shale, the Vanderbeeker family gathered in the living room for a family meeting. Their pets—a dog named Franz, a cat named George Washington, and a house rabbit named Paganini—sprawled on the carpet, taking afternoon naps in a strip of sunlight. The pipes rumbled companionably within the brownstone walls.

"Do you want the good news or the bad news first?"

The five Vanderbeeker kids looked at their parents.

"Good news," said Isa and Laney.

"Bad news," said Jessie, Oliver, and Hyacinth.

"Right-o," said Papa. "Good news first." He paused and adjusted his glasses. "You kids all know how much Mama and I love you, right?"

Oliver, who was nine years old and wise to the ways of the world, put down his book and squinted. "Are you guys getting divorced? Jimmy L's parents got a divorce. Then they let him get a pet snake." He kicked the backs of his sneakers against the tall stack of ancient encyclopedias he was sitting on.

"No, we're—" Papa began.

"Is it true?" six-year-old Hyacinth whispered, tears pooling in her round eyes.

"Of course we're—" Mama said.

"What's a dorce?" interrupted Laney, who was four and three-quarters years old and practicing her forward rolls on the carpet. She was wearing an outfit of red plaids, lavender stripes, and aqua polka dots that she had matched herself.

"It means Mama and Papa don't love each other anymore," said twelve-year-old Jessie, glaring at her parents from behind chunky black eyeglasses. "What a nightmare."

"We'll have to split our time between them," added Isa, Jessie's twin. She was holding her violin, and jabbed her bow against the arm of the couch. "Alternating holidays and summers and whatnot. I think I'm going to be sick."

Mama threw up her hands. "STOP! Just . . . everyone, please. Stop. Papa and I are not getting a divorce. Absolutely not. We're going about this all wrong." Mama glanced at Papa, took a deep breath, and briefly closed her eyes. Isa noticed dark circles under her mom's eyes that hadn't been there the week before.

Mama's eyes opened. "Let's start over. First, answer this question: on a scale of one to ten, how much do you like living here?"

The Vanderbeeker kids glanced around at their home, a brownstone in Harlem, New York City. It consisted of the basement; a ground floor with a living room that flowed into an open kitchen, a bathroom, and a laundry room; and a first floor with three bedrooms, a walk-in-closet-turned-bedroom where Oliver lived, and another bathroom, all lined up in a row. A door on the ground floor opened up to a skinny backyard, where a mommy cat and her new litter of kittens made their home under a hydrangea bush.

The kids considered Mama's question.

"Ten," Jessie, Isa, Hyacinth, and Laney replied.

"A million," said Oliver, still squinting suspiciously at his parents.

"It's the best place in the world," reported Laney, who somersaulted again and knocked down Isa's music stand. The pets scattered, except Franz, who didn't flinch, despite now being covered in sheet music.

"We've lived here most of our lives," said Isa. "It's the perfect home."

"Except the Beiderman, of course," added Jessie. The Beiderman lived on the brownstone's third floor. He was a seriously unpleasant man. He was also their landlord.

"*Mr.* Beiderman," Papa corrected Jessie. "And funny you mention him." Papa stood up and started pacing the length of the couch. His face was so grim that his ever-present smile creases disappeared. "I didn't see this coming, but Mr. Beiderman just told me he's not renewing our lease."

"He's not renewing our—" Jessie started.

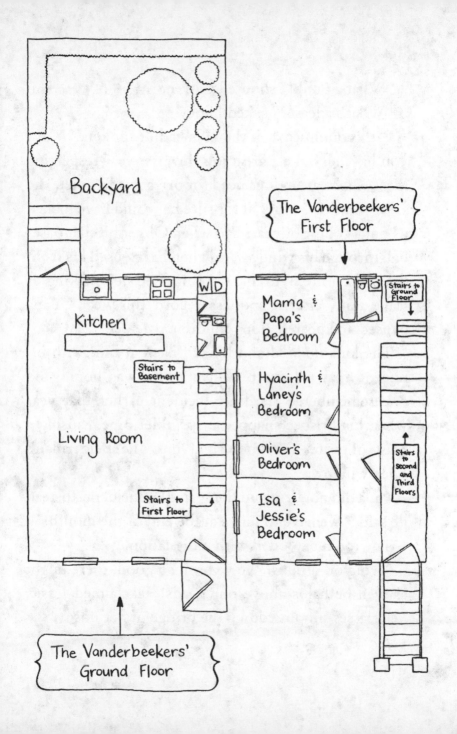

"What a punk!" shouted Oliver.

"What's a lease?" asked Laney.

Papa continued as if the kids hadn't spoken. "Now, you have all done a great job this past year respecting Mr. Beiderman and his need for privacy and quiet," he said. "I mean, I thought for sure he would have kicked us out a couple of years ago when Oliver hit that baseball through his window, or when Franz used his front door like a fire hydrant. I'm surprised he's making us leave now, after a spotless record this year." Papa paused and peered at his children.

The kids nodded and looked back at him with innocent eyes, all except Oliver, who was hoping no one remembered the little incident earlier that year when his Frisbee snapped a sprinkler pipe, causing a blast of water to shoot right into the Beiderman's open window.

Papa did not bring up the sprinkler incident. Instead he said, "We have to move at the end of the month."

The room exploded with indignation.

"Are you *serious*? We've been so good, there might as well be halos above our heads!" exclaimed Jessie, her glasses slipping down the bridge of her nose.

"I haven't bounced a basketball in front of the building in months!" Oliver said.

"What's a lease?" Laney asked again.

"Isa has to practice violin in the freaking dungeon!" said Jessie.

"Language," Mama warned at the same time Isa said, "I *like* practicing down there."

Papa looked at Laney. "We have a lease with Mr. Beiderman. It's an agreement between us for living here."

Laney considered what Papa said as she prepped another somersault. "So that means he doesn't want us?"

"It's not that . . ." Mama trailed off.

"I think the Beetleman needs hugs," Laney decided. She completed an accident-free somersault, then rolled over to lie on her stomach, searching for her bunny, who had taken refuge under the couch.

Jessie glanced at the calendar on the wall. "So that's it? We've only got eleven days left here?"

"He's really going to make us move right after Christmas?" asked Isa.

"Is it because I can't keep Franz quiet?" asked Hyacinth as she chewed her fingernails. When Franz heard

Hyacinth say his name, his tail gave a little wag and his eyes fluttered open, then drifted closed again.

"I think it's my fault," Isa said.

Her siblings stared at her. No one could imagine perfect Isa ever being the cause of getting kicked out of their home.

"You know, because of my violin playing."

"Kids, it's no one's fault," Mama interjected. "Remember how Papa and Uncle Arthur installed those energy-saving windows last year? Those windows are much more soundproof than the old ones. We've done all we can to try to persuade Mr. Beiderman to let us stay. I even left a box of lavender macarons outside his door." Mama blinked rapidly. As a professional pastry chef, she took macarons very seriously.

"What a waste," grumbled Oliver, who also took macarons very seriously.

"Will our new place have a basement? So I can practice?" Isa asked.

"I'm only moving if I can have a science lab in the new place. With a Bunsen burner. And new Erlenmeyer flasks," Jessie said stubbornly.

"My room's going to look exactly the same, right? Like, *exactly*?" asked Oliver.

"Will we move close by? So Franz can keep all his doggie friends?" asked Hyacinth. At Hyacinth's comment, the other kids' eyes widened. They'd never considered that they might have to leave the neighborhood where they knew everyone on the block by name, age, and hairstyle.

"I've lived in this neighborhood my whole life," Papa said. "My job is here." Only Hyacinth noticed that he didn't answer her question or look anyone in the eye when he said that. "Listen, kids, I have to fix the wobbly banister on the second floor and then take the building trash out. But we're not done talking about this, okay?"

Papa took his worn blue coveralls off the coat hanger and pulled them over the work clothes he was wearing for his computer repair job; the coveralls looked like something an auto mechanic would wear. Papa observed the somber faces of his kids. "I'm really sorry about this. I know you love this place. But I promise, this will turn out okay." He slipped out the door.

The kids hated when their parents talked about things turning out okay. How could they know? Before the kids could start in with the questions again, Mama's cell phone pinged. She glanced at the caller, then back at the kids. "I have to get this. But . . . don't worry. We'll talk about it more, I promise!" The kids watched her rush up the stairs, then heard her say, "Yes, Ms. Mitchell, thank you for calling. We're *very* interested in that apartment you listed—" followed by her bedroom door shutting.

"Move!" said Oliver, breaking the silence. "That's bananas! Rotten Beiderman."

"I can't imagine *not* living here," Isa said, her fingers running over her violin strings. "I really hope it wasn't my violin playing that caused all this."

Isa had discovered Mr. Beiderman's particular distaste for instruments six years ago, when she was in first grade. She was performing "Twinkle, Twinkle, Little Star" on her tiny, one-eighth-sized instrument for their second-floor neighbor, Miss Josie. Isa stood outside Miss Josie's apartment, but halfway through her song, Mr. Beiderman's door on the third floor burst open. He yelled down the staircase for the terrible racket to stop or he would call the police. Then the door slammed.

The police! On a six-year-old violinist! Isa was in tears, and Miss Josie invited her in and fed her cookies from a delicate china dish and gave her a pretty lace handkerchief to dry her eyes. Then Miss Josie insisted that Isa keep the handkerchief, which Isa to this day stowed in her violin case.

"It makes no sense," said Jessie, pacing back and forth between the couch and the picture window. She ran her hands through her wild hair, which made her look like a crazed scientist. "Newton's third law says that for every action there is an equal and opposite reaction. Now consider this: Papa does so much for the building. He keeps the front stoop clean, he rakes leaves, he shovels snow. He saves the Beiderman so much money by doing all the repairs himself. So what about Newton's third law? The Beiderman kicking us out of the building is *not* an equal reaction."

"I want to see a Newton!" exclaimed Laney.

"I don't think that law applies here," said Isa, unconsciously adjusting her neat ponytail into an even neater ponytail.

"Newton's laws apply to everything," Jessie said with her I'm-right-and-no-one-can-convince-me-otherwise voice.

"Uncle Arthur helps with the big repairs," Oliver commented as he searched through the stack of ancient encyclopedias for the one marked with an *N*.

"Papa does all the daily stuff," Jessie pointed out. "And he fixes Uncle Arthur's laptop whenever it breaks."

Oliver pulled the correct encyclopedia from the stack and flipped through it. "Newton is this guy," he said to Laney, pointing to a photo in the book.

"He has *very* nice hair," said Laney, running her fingers over the picture.

"Don't read that," scolded Jessie. "Those books are sixty years old and full of inaccurate science."

"Okay, people," Isa interrupted. "Let's get back on topic. I figure we have until Christmas to convince the Beiderman to let us stay."

"That's only four and a half days!" Jessie exclaimed. She looked at her watch. "One hundred and six hours."

"Exactly. Less than five days, people. Who has ideas?"

"Give him lots of hugs?" suggested Laney.

Oliver rubbed his hands together and raised one eyebrow. "Let's spray-paint his door." He gave a dramatic pause. "With disgusting bathroom words."

Isa ignored her brother. "Laney, I think you're right. We *should* try to do nice things for the Beiderman. You know, change his mind about us."

Jessie and Oliver looked skeptical. Hyacinth looked scared. Laney looked ready to give out hugs. Lots of hugs.

After a long silence, Oliver shrugged. "I'd be willing to do nice things for him. *If* he lets us stay."

"I guess I can try to be nice to him," Jessie said. Isa gave her a grateful look. "Although if this doesn't work, Oliver and I totally get to spray-paint his door. What do you think, Hyacinth?"

"He scares me," Hyacinth said, chewing at her pinky finger.

"It's five against one!" said Oliver. "What could he do to us, anyway?"

"I know you can do this," Isa said to Hyacinth. "You need to channel Hyacinth the Brave."

Hyacinth nodded but continued gnawing on her pinky.

Isa mused. "Wouldn't it be great if we were able to convince the Beiderman to let us stay? It would be like giving Mama and Papa the most amazing Christmas present ever."

The Vanderbeeker kids thought about giving their parents the Best Christmas Present Ever. Of course, Hyacinth had already made presents for them—she had completed them two months ago—but she liked the idea of a group gift. Oliver, who had spent quite a bit of time contemplating what he was going to *get* for Christmas, just remembered he was expected to *give* gifts as well.

"Mama and Papa deserve an amazing present from us," Oliver decided. "Let's keep it a secret."

Isa looked at him. "You haven't gotten them anything yet, have you?"

Oliver quickly changed the topic. "If it's a secret, we need to make sure you-know-who doesn't spill the beans." He gave a not-so-discreet nod toward Laney.

"Laney, this is a secret," instructed Jessie.

"Right," Laney agreed promptly.

"Right what?" Jessie said.

"Right, let's be nice to Beegermack," Laney said.

"Yes, but we're going to keep it a secret from Mama and Papa. Right, Laney?" Jessie prompted.

"Right!"

The five kids started exchanging ideas for winning over the man on the third floor. Operation Beiderman had officially begun.

They tried to feel hopeful about their plan, but in the back of each of their minds, they were all thinking the same thing: How do you make friends with a man you have never seen and who has not left his apartment in six years?

Two

The northern side of 141st Street was buffered by brownstones standing shoulder to shoulder, as if marching in formation. The buildings were all about the same height, with a ground floor (called the garden level) and three more floors rising above. Some brownstones, like the one the Vanderbeekers lived in, also had a basement, which Jessie referred to as the dungeon.

Although all the brownstones on the narrow, tree-lined street were the same size, each one had its own personality. One brownstone was rotund—like a jolly, well-fed grandfather—with a curved façade and decorative curlicues above round, owlish windows. A few skips down stood a perfectly symmetrical brownstone with a more regal disposition, which stood in direct contrast to its frivolous neighbor, a brownstone with flashy turrets and multicolored shingles that sparkled on sunny days.

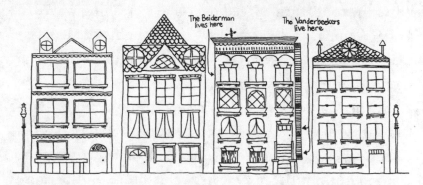

On the southern side of the street were a mix of larger apartment buildings, and at either end of the block were churches that had recently celebrated their centennials. Next to one of the churches sat a narrow piece of abandoned land, which Miss Josie always talked about making into a community garden and Oliver wanted converted into a basketball court. Two blocks to the west was a thin sliver of a park built into a rocky hill. At the top of the hill was a series of castle-like structures that made up the City College of New York's Harlem campus.

The sidewalks of 141st Street were wide, but the street was narrow. Majestic street lamps were staggered on both sides of the sidewalk, spaced fifty paces apart. The posts stretched past the first floor of the brownstone, then curved over like a crashing wave. In the evening, the warm glow of the lights made passersby feel that this street might have looked the same one hundred years earlier.

The Vanderbeekers' home—a humble red brownstone with a weathervane that spun on windy days—sat in the exact middle of the street. The brownstone stood out not because of its architecture, but because of the constant hum of activity that burst out of it. Among the many people who had visited the Vanderbeeker household there was quite a bit of debate about what it was like, but general agreement about what it was NOT:

Calm
Tidy
Boring
Predictable

At the moment, the things the Vanderbeeker household were NOT seemed more pronounced than usual. The kids had relocated their Beiderman meeting to Jessie and Isa's bedroom upstairs, where the ancient radiator whistled cheerfully at their arrival. Isa pulled out the easel and stood ready to jot notes, marker in hand. Hyacinth was making Operation Beiderman buttons for the kids to wear for their brainstorming sessions. Laney had discovered a box of flower clips under Isa's bed and was attaching each one to her ponytail.

As the kids settled in, Isa looked out at her siblings. As a biracial family, the kids exhibited an eclectic mix of physical characteristics and loved comparing which traits they got from what parent. Isa inherited her mother's stick-straight black hair, which Isa always wore in a sleek ponytail or an elegant French braid, while her twin Jessie had Papa's wild, untamable hair, which she never bothered to do anything with. Oliver had Papa's unruly hair but Mama's dark eyes. Hyacinth got Mama's nimble fingers but Papa's large feet. Laney was an exact blend of both of her parents; her hair was a shade of dark brown you would get if you swirled her parents' hair colors together on an artist's palette, her feet not small or large, and her eyes were darker than her papa's but lighter than her mama's.

Isa cleared her throat and tapped her marker on the easel. After the room quieted down and she called their meeting to order, she made the first Operation Beiderman suggestions.

"We could sing Christmas carols to him," she suggested. "You know, bring him a little Christmas spirit."

"What if he's Jewish? Would Christmas carols offend him?" asked Jessie from her spot by the radiator.

"We could sing Christmas *and* Hanukkah songs," said Isa.

"I have a little dreidel, I made it out of clay," sang Laney, off-key and very loud. Her head looked like a garden, with the flower clips attached all over it.

Oliver stuck fingers in his ears and winced. "That is just really, really bad."

"Maybe no dreidel songs," Isa said as Laney continued chanting, *"Dreidel, dreidel, dreidel, I made it out of clay!"*

"I have a feeling he won't want us singing to him," said Jessie, glancing at Laney. "I don't know, it's just a hunch."

"*Dreidel, dreidel, dreidel!*" Laney sang.

Isa put a hand over Laney's mouth to muffle her singing. "How about doing something to help around the building, like planting flowers or something? Miss Josie can help. She's great with flowers."

"It's winter. Flowers aren't going to grow now," Jessie said matter-of-factly.

"How about poinsettias? That's a holiday-ish flower," said Isa.

Hyacinth wrapped protective arms around Franz, who was sitting at her feet, and glared at Isa. "*Poinsettias* are poisonous to animals."

"What about wreaths?" Isa said.

"Too expensive," said Oliver.

Jessie huffed in frustration. "Okay, I see multiple problems." She ticked them off on her fingers. "One—he doesn't like us. Two—we have no money. Three—none of us has actually seen or met the Beiderman and we know nothing about him. Four—

he doesn't want to be disturbed. Five—he doesn't like us."

"That's the thing," said Isa. "I'm sure there's a way to show him that us living here is better than us *not* living here."

"Yeah, but how?" Jessie asked. "The only person we've ever seen go up there is the bird lady who drops off groceries once a week." The bird lady was aptly nicknamed; she resembled a crane, with her long, skinny legs and pointy beak nose.

Oliver shook his head. "She won't be any help. I said hi to her a few times and she walked past me like I wasn't even there. But I did peek into a grocery bag she left downstairs once. It was filled with frozen dinners."

"Yuck," said Hyacinth.

Jessie moved to her desk and switched on the computer she shared with Isa. "I'm going to see if I can find something out about him online." She tapped some keys, paused, then tapped more keys. "That's weird. I can't get online."

Oliver, who was used to the Internet shutting off at inconvenient times, jumped up. "I'll reset it."

His sisters heard him run down the hall, then some murmuring, then his feet stomping back to the twins' bedroom.

"Internet is shut off," Oliver announced with a scowl on his face. "Mama said they had to disconnect it today or pay for the whole next month plus a contract renewal fee."

"Oh great," Jessie said. "That's just perfect."

Isa sensed discontent brewing in the room. "Maybe we need some time to get our best ideas together." She capped her marker and shoved the blank easel back to the corner of the room. Isa stood up straight and tried to make her voice sound positive and cheerful. "Let's meet again after dinner. Everyone bring at least two awesome ideas. I know we can do it!"

Her siblings exchanged a look as they left the bedroom. When Isa did that falsely cheery voice thing, it meant she was worried.

Very worried.

❖ ❖ ❖

The Vanderbeeker kids spent the next few hours agonizing over the Beiderman dilemma. How could they convince him to change his mind? After all, it was only five days until Christmas.

Oliver had dark thoughts about the Beiderman as he banged down the stairs, grabbed his puffy jacket, and stepped out into the backyard. It was a space eclipsed by a century-old maple tree that dropped mountains of leaves every year from October to December. Oliver leaped onto the rope swing hanging from one of the many branches. He climbed up the rope so his feet rested on the fat knot at the bottom, and he got the rope swaying. As he gained momentum and height, he closed his eyes and breathed in the crisp cold air. He could almost smell the salty ocean wind. For that moment, he was hanging from the ropes of a pirate ship, racing across seas to confront and challenge the evil Beiderman, a peg-legged man with a long scar on his right cheek who was intent on destruction and mayhem.

In the midst of a nasty gale, he heard Jimmy L yelling at him. Oliver opened his eyes and looked over at the brownstone across the yard, where his friend was waving from his bedroom window on the second floor. Oliver waited for the rope to steady, then ascended the rope Navy SEAL–style by locking it between his feet and squatting and stepping all the way up to the top. He had learned this technique from his PE teacher, Mr. Mendoza—the most awesome human being ever to walk on the planet—who used to be a Navy SEAL himself and now challenged each of his students to climb a rope as fast as he could.

The top of the rope led to the start of the tree plank Uncle Arthur had made for him last year. Papa was hopeless with larger-scale construction projects and big repairs, so Uncle Arthur usually did those things for him.

Oliver hopped onto the sun-warmed plank. He scared off a squirrel that was sitting on the lid of the wood bin that held all his stuff; then he opened the lid and rummaged through the contents. There was a pack of spare batteries, a flashlight, a handful of granola bars, a first-aid kit (his Uncle Arthur insisted), and two bottles of orange Fanta that Oliver had to hide from his mother. At last he found what he was looking for: the walkie-talkie he shared with Jimmy L. The walkie-talkies were very useful since neither his nor Jimmy L's parents let them have cell phones. Oliver clicked the walkie-talkie on and the radio buzzed to life.

Oliver heard static; then Jimmy L's voice came through the device. "Captain Kidd, come in. Over."

"Magic Jay, this is Captain Kidd," Oliver responded. Magic Jay, Jimmy L's secret agent name, was riffed from his favorite basketball player, the legendary Magic Johnson. Captain Kidd was taken from the notorious pirate.

Oliver heard Jimmy L sigh through the walkie-talkie. "Captain Kidd, you need to say, 'Go Ahead.'"

"Oh yeah. Sorry. Magic Jay, go ahead."

"All quiet here. Over."

"Potential disastrous situation here at one-seven-seven West One-Four-One Street," Oliver said. "Immediate attention required. How copy?"

"Captain Kidd, I copy that. Elaborate. Over."

"The Beiderman—you know, our landlord?—he's forcing us to move. We have to leave by the end of the month. Over."

There was a long pause. Oliver pressed the button to talk again. "Magic Jay, radio check. Over."

Jimmy L's voice came through the device, loud enough to make the squirrel that was attempting a granola bar theft scurry away. "Are you *serious,* Oliver?"

Oliver grimaced. Jimmy L had broken conversation protocol, which had never happened before in the history of their walkie-talkie relationship.

"Yeah. My parents just told us," Oliver said into his device.

"This is the neighbor dude who yelled at your dad when we hit the baseball into his window?"

"That's the one," Oliver replied.

"That's so wrong, man. He can't take away your home."

"He's doing it. Papa says we're staying in the neighborhood, though."

"What about the treehouse? What about our walkie-talkies, man! We saved up for two months for these things."

"We're trying to convince the Beiderman to let us stay," Oliver said lamely. That head-squeezing feeling he had felt back when his parents first told him the news had returned.

"Let me know what happens, man. I can help you. Over."

Jimmy L was back to the walkie-talkie protocol, which Oliver took as a good sign. "Thanks. We on for basketball on Sunday? Over."

"Yeah, man. Current ETA for basketball game on Sunday is fourteen hundred hours. How copy?"

"Magic Jay, I copy that. Over."

"And, Oliver?"

"Yeah?"

"I really don't want you to move."

Oliver looked over at Jimmy L's window, but his friend had disappeared from view. The sun dropped behind a building, and a shadow fell across the tree-house. "Magic Jay, I read you loud and clear. Over."

Three

Hyacinth always had her best ideas when surrounded by her favorite things: scraps of odd-shaped fabric, buttons of many shapes, fat spools of thread in a rainbow of colors, and paper packets with deadly-looking sewing needles. Hyacinth's yellow paisley dress—her own creation—was made from an old pillowcase with holes cut out for her arms and head. She knotted a wide lavender ribbon around her waist to complete the look.

Sitting in the middle of the living room, Hyacinth rummaged through her ribbon collection as she tried to think of something to make for the Beiderman. It would have to be something so spectacular that he would change his mind about forcing them to move.

When Franz ambled by, Hyacinth took out a piece of green ribbon and draped it over him. His tail wagged, about a 200 on the wpm, or wags per minute, meter.

Out of the corner of her eye, Hyacinth spotted her mom leave the kitchen, disappear into the laundry room, then reappear lugging a stack of collapsed boxes that had been stored behind the washing machine. But they weren't just regular boxes. They were moving boxes.

Hyacinth's bleak mood was interrupted by Franz's happy yowl, followed by the sound of the mail slot opening and a stack of envelopes and magazines dropping onto the floor. Hyacinth hopped to her feet and followed Franz to the front door. She rotated the locks and pulled the door open.

"Hello, Mr. Jones!" said Hyacinth. Mr. Jones had been a postman in her neighborhood since before Papa was born. Franz barked twice and snuffled his nose into the mailbag.

"My friends!" Mr. Jones replied, rubbing Franz behind the ears with one hand and giving Hyacinth a high five with the other. He gently nudged Franz's nose out of the way, then took a biscuit from his mailbag and tossed it to him. Franz swallowed it whole and shamelessly rummaged through the mailbag for more.

Mr. Jones was dressed in his usual navy blue parka with the USPS sonic eagle logo, blue pants, black slip-resistant shoes (Mama had bought those for him after Mr. Jones slipped on a patch of ice last winter and sprained his wrist), and a fur cap (also with the sonic eagle logo). Mr. Jones wore a few accessories not sanctioned by the USPS. These were round buttons designed by Hyacinth with help from her button machine. One said "Mail Rules!" Another said "Love Your Postman," and the last said "Dogs Are a Postman's Best Friend." The dog one was the hardest to read, given the amount of text squeezed onto the tiny circle.

"And how are we doing today, Miss Hyacinth?" Mr. Jones said.

"We are fine, thank you," Hyacinth said in her most polite voice.

"Isn't that so nice to hear," Mr. Jones said as he took out a handkerchief and polished the three buttons attached to his parka. "Very nice to hear indeed."

Hyacinth picked up a small bag of bone-shaped dog treats from the table next to the door and handed them to Mr. Jones. "These are peanut butter dog treats," Hyacinth said. "If you haven't visited Señor Paz yet, I think he would like them." Señor Paz was an ancient black Chihuahua that lived down the street.

"I'm sure Señor Paz will right appreciate these," Mr. Jones replied, tucking the bag carefully into his pocket. He said *sure* the same way Hyacinth said *shore*. "As a matter of fact," he continued, "I'm heading that way next. Tell me now, did you make these by yourself?"

"Yes, I did," Hyacinth replied, glad he asked. She normally did not offer up this type of information, in case it was considered bragging. "Mama helped, of course."

"Your mama sure does have a hand with the baking," Mr. Jones said with an agreeable nod. "I don't know what the neighborhood dogs would do without you, Miss Hyacinth. I thought Snuggles had gone to heaven when he tasted the other dog cookie you made."

Thinking about Snuggles made Hyacinth think about her blanket (also named Snuggles), which made her think of her bed and bedroom, which reminded her of the move. "Oh, Mr. Jones! Mama and Papa told us the worst news ever today. We're moving!" She pulled at the hems of her shirtsleeves and balled the ends into her fists.

Mr. Jones's body appeared to shrink a few inches. "Move? What move?"

At that exact moment, Mama skidded into the foyer holding a bag. "Hello!" she said with a big, apologetic smile. "Hello, Mr. Jones! I baked some cookies. Would you like some? Nothing like double chocolate pecan cookies to comfort the tummy and the soul, I always say."

Mr. Jones did not reach out for the bag. "Now tell me straight, Mrs. Vanderbeeker. Are you moving?"

Hyacinth noticed that Mama also seemed to shrink a little bit. "Oh, Mr. Jones! I was hoping to tell you first. Our landlord isn't renewing our lease. We just found out."

"I've known your husband since he was born," Mr. Jones said, accusation in his eyes.

"I know, Mr. Jones. You're like a part of our family," Mama said, tears coming into her eyes as she nudged Franz's nose out of the mailbag and tucked the bag of double chocolate pecan cookies in there instead.

"We're looking for another place in the neighborhood, Mr. Jones. If you hear of anything, please let us know," Mama said.

Mr. Jones went quiet for a few seconds, then said, "Mr. Beiderman is your landlord?"

Hyacinth and Mama nodded.

Mr. Jones shook his head and glanced up, as if he expected to see Mr. Beiderman hanging out his third-floor window at that exact moment.

"Mr. Beiderman had some hard times," Mr. Jones said, looking back at them. "Hard times. He bought this brownstone a few months before your family moved in. He used to live a couple blocks away, right by the college. He worked there."

"You *knew* Mr. Beiderman? What did he do?" Hyacinth asked.

"He taught in the art history department."

"He made paintings?"

"He studied art and its history. Who made the art, where and when the artists lived, what techniques they used. Then he taught students about it," Mr. Jones said, giving Franz a final head pat.

"Well, I best be going. Lots of mail to deliver." Mr. Jones held up the bag Hyacinth had given him. "And dog treats to pass out. Have a good day, now." He tipped his fur cap and leaned slightly on the bar of his postage cart as he rolled it away from the Vander-beeker brownstone and down the street. Mama reached over Hyacinth's head and clicked the door closed, then shuffled back to the kitchen to cook dinner while Hyacinth watched out the window until she couldn't see Mr. Jones anymore.

✣ ✣ ✣

Laney—the youngest Vanderbeeker—had trans-formed into her alter ego, Panda-Laney. A furry white coat was draped over her stout body and she was crawling around, keeping her mama company in the kitchen. She was the only one who was not so con-cerned about the possibility of moving. If the Beider-man was the only obstacle, Laney knew she could win him over. She loved people! Surely he would love her too.

So instead of thinking about ideas to save their home like Isa had asked, Laney put all her attention on getting double chocolate pecan cookies from Mama. On occasion she pawed at Mama's feet and was rewarded with a carrot. Laney didn't like carrots so much—too crunchy and too orange—but Panda-Laney loved them! Panda-Laney also loved cookies—well, Laney liked them too—and if she was lucky and ate three whole carrots, usually a cookie would follow.

Panda-Laney peered around the kitchen island. She spied Paganini, her lop-eared bunny, under the couch.

"Paganini!" Panda-Laney said in a loud whisper. One bunny ear twitched, and Paganini's nose moved up and down like a motor. The gray rabbit scooted out from under the couch, and—after a suspicious glance in Franz's direction—hopped toward Panda-Laney's outstretched hand. Paganini loved it when Panda-Laney came out to play, because that meant carrots. After grabbing the carrot, Paganini dragged it back under the couch and devoured his prize.

Panda-Laney ate the other two carrots with less enthusiasm, then crawled back to her mom's heels and looked up.

"Okay, you little beggar!" Mama said with a smile. "Just one cookie, and bring one to your sister." Her mom passed her two cookies. Panda-Laney inspected both with a critical eye. One was a little bit larger, but the other was shaped like Paganini. Panda-Laney debated between them before choosing the larger one and giving the Paganini-shaped cookie to Hyacinth, who crammed it in her mouth and mumbled a gloomy "Thanks" without bothering to look up from her ribbons.

❁ ❁ ❁

Jessie, wearing jeans and a baggy navy hoodie, was perched on the steps leading to the dungeon with a pile of colored gumdrops and wooden toothpicks in neat piles around her. She was constructing model molecules by connecting colored gumdrops that were supposed to represent atoms, but she got distracted pretending the gumdrops were the Beiderman's eyes and she was stabbing them with the toothpicks.

Isa was down in the basement, positioned at the bottom of the stairs so she could see Jessie. Her violin was cradled on her shoulder and she was zipping through various etudes—short study pieces her music teacher insisted she practice every day. When she finished, she gazed up at Jessie.

"So . . . do you have any ideas for saving our home yet?" asked Isa.

Jessie scowled. "Does it look like I have any ideas? Can't you tell I'm in the anger stage of grief?"

"Jess, you've got to pull it together. We need your problem-solving brains."

Jessie put down her toothpicks and looked down the stairs. "Sorry. I'll totally have ideas when we meet up later."

Mama walked by and ruffled Jessie's already disheveled hair. "Ideas for what?" she asked.

"Oh. Uh, ideas for . . ." Jessie trailed off and looked down at Isa in alarm.

"Christmas Eve dinner," Isa lied.

"I'm so glad you girls are taking care of that," Mama said briskly. "And don't worry about what everyone has been saying. I'm sure it will be great. Why don't you look up some recipes online? I saw this one recipe for shredded Brussels sprouts with maple hickory nuts that maybe you want to try . . ." Mama passed Jessie her smartphone. "It's bookmarked under *Recipes.*"

Isa shuddered at the thought of Brussels sprouts—shredded or not—and Jessie made a face at the complexity of the recipe.

The twins had been responsible for preparing the family meal on Tuesdays since they turned twelve earlier that year. This year, Christmas Eve fell on a Tuesday, and in the Vanderbeeker tradition, Christmas Eve dinner rivaled Thanksgiving dinner in scope and quality. Oliver—not a huge believer in the twins' cooking abilities—suggested that Jessie and Isa have immunity on Christmas Eve, or perhaps that they trade for a different, less important day. Hyacinth agreed with Oliver's suggestion, and even Papa seemed inclined to think this was a good idea. The twins, offended by the little faith of their so-called family, insisted on keeping to the schedule and vowed to prove themselves.

That is, until they received the news about moving.

"It's going to be the worst Christmas Eve dinner if we have to move," grumbled Isa.

"Any ideas for what we should make? And not that Brussels sprouts thing," Jessie added.

Isa paused. "Anything but turkey. I'm still recovering from Thanksgiving. I will, I repeat, *will*, throw up."

"Okay, how about this." Jessie set aside the octane gumdrop molecule she had started on and grabbed a piece of paper and a pen. She settled back down on the top step. "We could do roasted vegetables for the side dish. We've never messed those up before." At Isa's nod, Jessie wrote "roasted vegetables" on the list. "Okay, main dish. What about beef stew? How hard could that be?" Isa nodded again, and Jessie jotted it down. "And what to conclude the meal with . . ." Jessie murmured to herself. She opened up the search engine on Mama's smartphone and scrolled through some recipes on the cooking website they liked to use. She picked two under the heading *Easy Dessert Recipes Sure to Impress Your Guests.* "What do you think about strawberry cheesecake and carrot cake?"

"Great," Isa said. "Add fresh bread from Castleman's Bakery too." Isa started a new etude, making a number of mistakes along the way.

"Okay." Jessie wrote the final menu on a sheet of paper.

The twins went on to the guest list. "Miss Josie and Mr. Jeet, of course," Isa said. "Oh man, what will *they* do if we move?" Miss Josie and Mr. Jeet had lived in the apartment above theirs for as long as anyone could remember. Retired, they spent a lot of time with the Vanderbeekers, and Mama and Papa helped them with grocery shopping and keeping track of their doctors' appointments and medicines.

"I don't think Laney and Hyacinth will be able to leave them," Jessie said. "Laney will latch herself on to Mr. Jeet's leg and refuse to let go."

Jessie continued with the guest list, which grew to include the children's favorite relatives, Auntie Harrigan and Uncle Arthur, who lived in Westchester, as well as Isa's music teacher, Mr. Van Hooten.

"Wouldn't it be amazing if we could get the Beiderman to come?" Isa mused.

"If the Beiderman ends up at our dinner table, it will be a Christmas miracle," replied Jessie.

Isa shrugged, then began playing "Csárdás" by Vittorio Monti, moving through to the end of the piece and striking the last note with a flourish of her bow. A familiar scuffling was heard outside. The door to the apartment burst open and in tumbled their dad.

Papa took off his coat and hung it up next to the door, then walked across the kitchen to the basement door. "Brava!" he called down to Isa. "A perfect rendition of 'Csárdás'! Excellent emotional interpretation! Amazing dynamics!"

"Oh, Papa." Isa rolled her eyes. "That was the worst!"

"But each time is new, my little violinist. You've never played it exactly that way, right? The beauty of live music!" He flicked a nickel down the staircase, where it bounced off some steps and landed in Isa's violin case, then he scooped up Laney and placed her on top of his shoulders. "Has anyone seen my Laney-Bean? I've been looking all over for her!"

"I'm not Laney-Bean. I'm Panda-Laney!" the white-swathed wonder called from above.

"Ah, Panda-Laney! My favorite type of panda! Let me see, I don't remember . . . Are Panda-Laneys . . . ticklish?" Laney collapsed in a torrent of giggles, and Papa swung her off his shoulders and to the ground. Laney wrapped her arms and legs around his left leg and held on for dear life. Papa half dragged her to where his wife was mixing batter for cheesy bread. The soup pot bubbled on the stove, the fragrant smell of herbs and vegetables drifting through the kitchen.

"Hello, beautiful lady," he said, dropping a kiss next to her ear.

Mama looked him over. Papa still wore his superintendent "uniform," an outfit of his own choosing that he insisted on wearing whenever he did building duties. "On the bright side," Mama said, "if we move, you won't have to wear that jumpsuit anymore."

"For your information," Papa said, both of his index fingers pointing down at his uniform, "these are *coveralls*. Only the coolest supers wear them."

"I want coveralls too," Laney said from the ground, where she still hung on to Papa's leg.

"See?" Papa said to Mama. "Our daughter has excellent taste."

"I just don't see why you can't wear your normal clothes to take out the trash," Mama said, pouring the bread batter into two greased loaf pans.

"Honey, I can't wear my *computer* clothes when I do stuff around the building. The computer clothes don't have the let's-get-dirty-and-fix-things personality that my coveralls do."

Mama sighed.

Papa scanned the living room and took in the funereal atmosphere. Isa played a mournful tune on her violin, and the brownstone was devoid of the bustle and laughter typical of the Vanderbeeker household. His voice lowered. "They're not taking the move well, are they?"

Mama looked into Papa's eyes. "No matter what happens," she said, touching his cheek, "I'm grateful for the past six years here." She paused. "Even if you did have to wear coveralls."

Papa's smile didn't change the melancholy in his eyes as he reached up to put his hand over hers. "Life here couldn't have been better."

Four

After Oliver's conversation with Jimmy L, he came back inside, swiped three of the double chocolate pecan cookies Mama had baked earlier, then retreated to his bedroom for some Beiderman brainstorming time.

Being the only boy among four sisters was not easy, but there was one perk: Oliver was the only one in the family who had a room to himself. Indeed, it was a tiny walk-in-closet-turned-bedroom, just big enough to hold his loft bed and a narrow desk underneath it. Five years ago, Uncle Arthur arrived unannounced wearing a tool belt and armed with a power drill. Uncle Arthur declared that if Oliver was to survive being the only boy among many sisters, he needed two things: an imagination and a place of his own to escape to. His uncle proceeded to install bookshelves on every inch of available open wall space in the room while Papa looked on in wonder at the blur of construction. From that day on, Uncle Arthur sent Oliver books on a monthly basis—books about superheroes and Greek mythology and pirates and space exploration and presidents. Now walking into Oliver's room was like entering a miniature library that someone happened to live in.

An hour later, Oliver had done zero brainstorming. Rather, he was so deep into his book, Robert Louis Stevenson's *Treasure Island*, that he didn't hear Mama calling him to dinner. He was Jim Hawkins, struggling to board the ship after cutting the anchor loose, only to be confronted by the wicked pirate Israel Hands—

"OLIVER!" his sisters yelled, crashing into his sacred, quiet bedroom.

Oliver jumped at the intrusion before realizing that one, he was not Jim Hawkins, and two, he was not on a pirate ship. He lifted the book right in front of his face. "Leave. Me. Alone."

Laney bunny-hopped over to Oliver and threw her arms around him. "I love you, Ollie," she declared, planting four wet kisses on his cheek. "Time for dinner!"

"Ugh," Oliver said, scrubbing his cheek with his sleeve. "Long John Silver would maroon you for such despicable behavior."

Laney grabbed Oliver's hand and tried to yank him to his feet, budging him not one bit. She did, however, manage to trip over his left knee and knock down a pile of comic books stacked by his desk.

Laney emerged from the comic-book avalanche still gripping Oliver's hand. "Come on! Dinnertime! Mama made *cheesy bread.*"

Oliver's stomach rumbled, the double chocolate pecan cookies he'd eaten an hour earlier a distant memory. Despite the lure of piracy, he decided that dinner would be a good idea. Together the Vanderbeeker children clambered down the steps to the kitchen, all talking at once.

"Ah, the sound of my graceful children coming down the stairs. Delightful," Papa called from the kitchen.

Mama turned toward her children and pointed a canary-yellow spatula with a glob of meringue cream at them. "Attention! I need this table set, *pronto!*" The meringue cream dripped off the spatula and splattered on the floor, right next to Franz, who was lurking around the kitchen hoping for such a miracle.

The kids rushed around, banging drawers and dropping utensils. Finally the table was set, food was placed in the middle, and people were seated. Then Oliver got up because he wanted ice in his water. Then Laney insisted on rummaging through the silverware drawer for her special soup spoon. When everyone was seated again, the family held hands, Papa said a quick blessing over the food, and dinner began.

"So," Oliver said, jumping right into the very topic at the forefront of everyone's minds. "I don't know about you, but I'm feeling like we need to *see* the Beiderman. You know, before we move." He looked at his parents with his "innocent" face.

Papa glanced at Mama. "He's trying to look innocent. Something's up."

Mama sighed and looked at Oliver. "What are you planning to do to that poor man?"

"What? Nothing! Why is everyone looking at me like that?" Oliver reached over the table and riffled through the slices of cheesy bread, searching for the biggest piece. "I'm just saying, the Beiderman should be a man and show his face to us at least one time before he evicts us. We need an *explanation!*"

"It's *Mr.* Beiderman, and he's not evicting us. He's not renewing our lease," Mama said.

Isa spoke up. "I've always wondered what he looks like. Is he short? Tall? What color hair does he have?"

"What types of things is he interested in?" Jessie chimed in.

"Does he like cute little bunnies?" asked Laney, bits of cheesy bread escaping from her mouth.

"What about Christmas carols? Or, do you know if he's Jewish?" asked Oliver. For that, he got a kick under the table from two different sources. Based on the synchronicity and the force of the kicks, he was pretty sure they came from the twins.

"I know absolutely nothing about him," Mama said. "You know how private he is."

"Every time I've had to go into his apartment," Papa said, "he tells me to let myself in with my super key and closes himself into his bedroom until I'm done."

"You have a *super key?*" said Laney, amazed. "Does it have powers? Is it magic?"

"He means the *superintendent* key," Oliver said, rolling his eyes.

"I think this whole situation is weird," Jessie said, banging her soup spoon on the table. "We've lived here for six years and haven't seen him once. Then he kicks us out of our home without even getting to know us?"

"Mr. Jones said he used to work at City College before we moved in," Hyacinth said.

Mama cleared her throat, then said the words no one wanted to hear. "We need to start packing tomorrow."

Around the table each Vanderbeeker finished dinner, but the food tasted like dust and left them empty and unsatisfied. After clearing the table and loading the dishwasher, the kids headed upstairs as the brownstone creaked mournfully in the silence.

✧ ✧ ✧

"Off to the REP?" asked Isa.

"Desperate times call for desperate measures," replied Jessie.

Isa opened her closet door, pulled out an armload of hoodies, and passed them out. While everyone zipped up the thick sweatshirts, Jessie gathered the REP bag, a duffel that was filled with fleece blankets along with a large two-liter bottle that used to hold soda water but was now filled with tap water. With what Oliver believed was superhuman strength, he yanked up the twins' bedroom window and the kids climbed out onto the fire escape. Isa hitched Laney on her back and started up the groaning metal stairs to the REP, otherwise known as the Roof of Epic Proportions.

There were two ways to get up to the REP, but the other way required the Vanderbeeker kids to use the ladder directly across from the Beiderman's door. They had never used that roof entrance, for obvious reasons.

"Be careful," Isa reminded them. She said that same thing, in her listen-to-me-or-else tone, every time they went to the roof. First, Isa and Laney passed Miss Josie and Mr. Jeet's living room. ("Hi, Miss Josie!" Laney chirped, tapping the window and waving when Miss Josie looked up from her television show.) Next, they crept past the Beiderman's windows, which were covered by blackout curtains. Finally, they emerged onto the roof.

The roof floor was not the typical concrete, sandpapery surface that covered most roofs in New York City. Right before the Vanderbeekers arrived, the one-hundred-year-old roof was replaced and then topped off with currant-colored ceramic tiles. The tiles made the rooftop welcoming and soundproof. Nevertheless, the kids knew to tread in the same manner they did when visiting one another's bedrooms late at night, being careful not to wake their parents. They were certain the Beiderman could not hear them, because he would definitely have said something about it. And not in a nice way, either.

"Water wall to launch, with your permission," Jessie said to Isa when she got to the roof, lifting the water bottle out of the REP bag and holding it up. The sky glowed a Persian blue, and the black silhouettes of the buildings gave the neighborhood a fantasy quality, like the chimney-sweep scene in the *Mary Poppins* movie.

"Go for it, boss," Isa replied, taking the REP bag from Jessie and setting the blankets out on the ground.

Jessie had built the water wall along the eastern façade of the brownstone, inspired by a science class during which her teacher showed them different cartoons of Rube Goldberg machines. The one Jessie loved the most was the cartoon demonstrating a sheet music turner. A guy who looked like a young Beethoven was sitting at a music stand, where he was pumping a foot pedal that set off a bunch of reactions, like starting a bike pump that puffed air into a boxing glove that punched a lever that caused a stick to shoot out and turn the page on the music stand. This comic gave Jessie an excellent idea for something to make for Isa, and when she couldn't get the sheet music turner to work, she created the water wall instead. It ended up being a present for Isa's twelfth birthday, and Jessie had spent nearly all of June working on it.

Jessie brought her water bottle over to the east side of the brownstone, where an industrial metal funnel rested on the roof ledge. Jessie carefully positioned the water bottle in the wire cage, aimed the spout into the base of the funnel, then unscrewed the bottle cap. The water flowed into the funnel, where it descended through a black hose and settled into a metal container

secured to the edge of the building. It then trickled along chutes that zigzagged along the side of the building, causing a series of water wheels with spokes to ping three sets of miniature wind chimes as they rotated.

Next, the water set off a lever attached to a wooden rain stick, nudging the rain stick to sway back and forth like a lazy seesaw. The water then came to a drop-off, where it waterfalled one story down to a rounded piece of tin that Jessie had found on the curb coming home from school one day. The tin was magic; it vibrated and produced a different sound depending on what angle the water hit it. Then the water rolled off right into Mama's herb garden and kept the plants hydrated during the growing season, which was probably the only reason she had let Jessie construct the water wall in the first place.

A two-liter bottle of water was enough to keep the water wall's music going for about fifteen minutes. The sound from the water wall was what Isa imagined a wind quartet would sound like if the musicians played on a grassy field on a rainy day (with umbrellas to protect the instruments, of course). Isa had been speechless when Jessie unveiled it on their birthday. Jessie had shrugged and said, "It's just physics, no big deal." The music was loud enough for the Vanderbeekers to hear from the roof but quiet enough not to penetrate the Beiderman's soundproof windows.

With the water wall singing, the Vanderbeekers gathered at the south side of the brownstone, leaning their elbows along the ledge (except Laney, who could only rest her fingertips on the ledge and had to be picked up by Isa so she could see over the wall). The south view was the best. From there they could see the rows of buildings up and down the block. In the distance, City College was lit up on the hill, looking like an ancient castle complete with turrets.

"Let's play 'listen without paying attention,'" suggested Laney. This was one of her favorite games—she had made it up herself—and it didn't make sense to the rest of the kids until they were in the middle of the game. Then it made perfect sense.

"Close your eyes," instructed Laney.

A few moments later, Hyacinth heard the sounds of merengue music coming from one of the apartments down the block. Oliver heard a sliding door opening and their next-door neighbor click a lighter for a cigarette. Jessie heard unrestrained laughter from a group of people walking down the street on the other side of the building. Isa heard the rain stick's pebbles shift back and forth on the water wall. Laney, whose eyes were squeezed as tight as she could squeeze them, tried not to hear anything. Still, she heard Miss Josie's rich voice singing a gospel tune. It was amazing what the Vanderbeekers could hear when they weren't trying to listen to anything.

Hyacinth's voice interrupted the not-listening. "Do you think we'll really stay in Harlem?"

"Of course," scoffed Jessie, opening her eyes. "Papa said so."

Hyacinth shook her head. "You know, he never really *said* we'd stay. And he looked sort of weird when he was talking about it. He had that same look he gets when he tells Grandma he loves that yucky anchovy casserole she always makes when she comes here."

"Papa has lived here all his life," Oliver said. "He's like the mayor of our block. He'd never leave."

"And his computer repair job is here," Jessie pointed out. "He said he would hire me as his assistant when I turn sixteen." Jessie paused for a nanosecond. "Only one thousand, two hundred and fifty-seven days to go."

"Papa doesn't lie," Laney said. "Lying is bad news."

"I agree, Laney." Isa looked out at the neighborhood. "This is my favorite view ever," she said.

"Do you think the Beiderman worked at the castle?" Hyacinth asked, looking at City College. "I thought only nice people were allowed to work in the castle."

"Princesses live there," Laney stated, bracing her arms on Isa's shoulders so she could get a better view.

"Princesses *do not* live there," Oliver said. "That's a college, dummy."

"Don't call your sister 'dummy,'" Hyacinth and Isa said in unison.

"Come on," Isa said. "We have work to do." She led her siblings to the blankets, where they sat down for the second meeting of Operation Beiderman. Hyacinth handed out the buttons she'd made, and her siblings attached them to their hoodies.

"Remember, not a word to Mama and Papa," Jessie reminded them. The Vanderbeeker kids formed a tight circle and did a communal fist bump.

"What if we fail?" asked Hyacinth.

"We won't," Oliver said, pulling out a startlingly realistic pirate sword that was attached to a belt loop on his jeans and lifting it high in the air. "My idea is for all of us to get swords—"

"So I've been thinking," Isa interrupted, "that the key to winning the Beiderman over is to play to our strengths."

"Good thing *I* have so many fine qualities to show off to the Beiderman," Oliver boasted.

"Who wants to share their ideas first?" asked Isa.

"Hyacinth should do the first Beiderman mission," Jessie said. "She's the craftiest person in the world."

Hyacinth froze, then shook her head in short, quick bursts.

"C'mon, Hyacinth! You're the perfect person to go first. Not too overwhelming"—here Jessie shot a glance at Laney, who was busy drawing hearts on everyone's hands with a felt-tip pen she had found in the REP bag—"and not too obnoxious." Here Jessie glared at Oliver, who was trying to untie Isa's sneakers with the tip of his sword.

"Hyacinth the Brave could totally do it," Isa suggested.

Hyacinth continued to shake her head.

"Since Hyacinth is out . . ." Isa said, surveying her siblings, "Jessie, you better go first."

"Why not you?" said Jessie.

"Because of our musical disagreements," replied Isa. Her siblings knew it was true. They all thought it was a shame the Beiderman reacted so strongly to stringed instruments, especially given Isa's extraordinary progress over the last six years. She had left the "scary, screechy" phase of violin playing shortly after that first year, and had even won a couple of violin competitions recently.

Jessie sighed. "Fine. Send me to my doom. But someone's coming with me."

"I'll help, I'll do it!" Laney yelled, waving an arm in the air.

"Shhh!" said Isa, Jessie, and Hyacinth.

"I'll help too," Oliver said.

Jessie looked over the two candidates. "Okay, Laney. You're in."

"Hey, what about me?" Oliver said.

"You're a little . . ." Jessie began.

"What?" demanded Oliver.

"Unpredictable," suggested Isa.

"Volatile," added Jessie.

Hyacinth didn't say anything, but she gazed at Oliver adoringly.

"I'm not that bad!" said Oliver.

"No, you're not—for a boy—but you could use some . . . finesse," said Jessie.

"Finesse," grumbled Oliver. "I have so much finesse, you don't even know."

※　※　※

The water wall had long stopped singing, and the sky had darkened to an endless black by the time the kids were finished bouncing ideas back and forth. It turned out that Oliver *did* have the best idea for the first Operation Beiderman. However, even Oliver ultimately agreed that he was not the best delivery person. In addition to the baseball and sprinkler incidents, Oliver felt the Beiderman had a particular dislike for him because he used to practice dribbling on the sidewalk in front of the brownstone. This bothered no one in the entire neighborhood . . . unless your name was Beiderman.

"Good idea, Oliver," Isa said as she packed up the REP bag. "I think this is going to work."

"See," Oliver said over his shoulder. He swaggered back to the fire escape, his pirate sword swinging from his belt loop. "I told you I got finesse."

Saturday, December 21

Five

The radiator woke Hyacinth the next day, whistling a joyful good morning. Instead of feeling cheered by it like she usually did, Hyacinth felt as if sewing needles were poking around in her stomach. It was Saturday, the official start to Operation Beiderman. Through her window she could see the last wrinkled leaves gripping the branches of the ancient red maple, refusing to drift down to the ground until absolutely necessary.

Hyacinth could tell Laney was still in a deep sleep without even looking at her. Laney made a funny whistling sound when she slept. Hyacinth climbed down from her bunk, shoved her feet into her bear slippers, and tugged on her favorite fuzzy sweatshirt, which she had stolen from Oliver. She stepped over a snoozing Franz and crept out the door, careful to turn the doorknob in that special way to keep it from squeaking.

Despite being second-to-last in the Vanderbeeker family line, Hyacinth often felt she was the true middle child. Of course, Oliver had earned that right by being born between two sets of sisters, but he had the honor of being the only boy, which held him apart. The twins were exactly the same age, so in Hyacinth's mind they sort of counted as one. If you didn't include Oliver because he was a boy, that left Hyacinth taking the true middle spot, fending for herself in a household of loud, strong-willed, attention-grabbing siblings.

To get her fair share of time with her parents, Hyacinth had developed the habit of getting up early. She tiptoed downstairs. Her dad was sitting on the couch, cradling his mug of steaming coffee, a thick book opened before him. Paganini was hopping in bizarre patterns around the living room carpet, periodically flinging himself into the air and spinning as if auditioning for a Broadway show. George Washington lay sprawled on his back, lazily swatting the bunny as he zipped past.

Hyacinth stepped around the animals and snuggled in next to her dad. He slipped his arm around her, drawing her close. He smelled like coffee and peppermint drops.

"Papa, why does the Beiderman hate us so much?" Hyacinth asked.

Papa kissed the top of Hyacinth's head. "*Hate* is such a strong word. I definitely don't think he hates you. I think he's unhappy, which has nothing to do with you kids."

Hyacinth thought about the Beiderman mission they had planned for that morning and was glad they were going to do something so nice for him. Then she felt ashamed that she was too afraid to do the first mission, even though all her siblings wanted her to.

"Papa?" asked Hyacinth.

"Yes?"

"How can I get more brave?" Hyacinth squeezed her eyes shut and curled in nearer to Papa. She was afraid he would tell her she would never be brave.

"Why, Hyacinth, you're one of the bravest people I know," Papa said.

"Really?" asked Hyacinth, her eyes popping open.

"Really," said Papa. "It takes a super-brave person to be as generous as you are, Hyacinth. Not many people are brave enough to be so loving."

Hyacinth thought about this while she watched Paganini nibble on a stack of books and George Washington groom his ears.

Papa smiled at the animals. "'Until one has loved an animal, a part of one's soul remains unawakened.'"

Hyacinth looked up at her father. "What does that mean, Papa?"

"It means that animals make our hearts happy in a very special way. A French man named Anatole France said that a long time ago."

The sound of a door opening, then another one, marked the end of Papa and Hyacinth's morning alone time. A faucet turned on in the upstairs bathroom, and they heard water whoosh through the pipes within the brownstone walls. A big thunk followed, which was most likely Oliver jumping off the last few ladder rungs of his loft bed.

Soft footsteps padded down the upstairs hallway and paused at the top of the stairs. Laney was awake. She descended one step at a time, the stairs creaking happily. When she got to the bottom, she speed-walked to Papa, climbed into his lap, and nuzzled in close.

And there they sat for a precious few minutes, Papa and his two youngest children, while the rest of the family awoke and the sounds of the city began its crescendo all around them.

❖ ❖ ❖

Ten minutes later, the Vanderbeeker apartment buzzed with kids and parents going in and out of bedrooms and bathrooms and up and down the stairs. When Isa came downstairs, she saw Oliver, his hair rumpled on one side, sitting slouched on a stool by the kitchen island, staring at an open book. She pulled out the stool across from him and sat down.

"Do you really think we can win the Beiderman over in four days?" she asked as she gathered her hair back and braided it in a long plait.

Oliver spoke without looking away from his book.

"Sure, and why don't we solve America's budget crisis and save the orcas while we're at it?"

Isa paused. "So . . . that's a no?"

"Honestly," Oliver said, "I have no idea."

"I think your idea was brilliant."

"Really?" Oliver perked up a bit.

"Oh yeah," Isa replied. "I have a good feeling about it."

"Then you should hear my *other* idea," said Oliver, closing his book. "I think we should use a combination of Laney, Hyacinth, and Jessie. First Jessie can pick the lock to the Beiderman's door. Next Hyacinth can torture him with her sewing needles. *Then* Laney can suffocate him with kisses and hugs until he—"

"Let's just hope the first idea works and he realizes how wonderful we are and begs us to stay," Isa interrupted.

Oliver grinned. "Too bad you're too nice. I could probably think of a way to get you in on the plan . . ."

While Oliver and Isa discussed the Beiderman mission, Hyacinth came downstairs with an armload of felt. She settled down on the living room carpet and busied herself cutting red felt circles for her holly berry placemats. Franz looked on with his woeful basset hound eyes, then went to his food bowl and began the slow process of nudging it across the room until it banged into her knee.

Hyacinth recognized the gravity of the situation immediately. "Oh, my poor Franz! You must be starving!"

Franz looked at Hyacinth and forgave her at once. Hyacinth filled his bowl with precisely one scoop of dry dog food. The veterinarian had warned her against giving Franz more than that for fear he would get too heavy. Oliver, who had been beside her at the appointment, muttered "Too late" under his breath, just loud enough for Hyacinth to hear. It was a particular gift of Oliver's that he could say things that adults couldn't hear but his sisters could.

Hyacinth was feeding Franz when a disheveled Jessie came downstairs with her signature bed head, followed by Laney wearing a glittery crown.

"We're off!" Jessie announced to Isa, Oliver, and Hyacinth as she wrangled Laney into her puffy purple jacket and sparkly winter boots.

"Make sure to buy extra cheese croissants," Oliver said.

"Good idea!" Jessie said as she grabbed a ragged scarf and wrapped it around her neck. "All the better to persuade the Beiderman with."

"The extra cheese croissants were for me," Oliver clarified. "But I guess you can get some for the Beiderman too."

Jessie and Isa shared an eye roll, then Jessie took Laney's hand and led her outside, where they promptly bumped into Mr. Smiley, the superintendent at the big apartment building on their block, and his daughter Angie, who was friends with Oliver.

"Hello, Laney! Hello, Jessie!" Mr. Smiley said.

"Tell Oliver he owes me a basketball game!" Angie said. Oliver and Angie were constantly challenging each other to one-on-one basketball games, and it had to be said that Angie was so good, the boys' basketball team *begged* her to play for them.

Jessie and Laney waved goodbye. They passed by the brownstone with the turrets, then the brownstone covered with ivy, then the brownstone where garlands of pine were draped along all the windows and a huge wreath with a wavy burgundy bow decorated the heavy wooden door. They turned the corner onto the boulevard, where the quiet of their street gave way to city buses with their screeching brakes and shop owners unlocking and rolling up the metal grates they had pulled down over their stores the night before. A garbage truck squealed to a stop down the street, and Mark, one of their neighborhood sanitation men, jumped off the back and tossed the contents of an overflowing trash bin into the hopper of the garbage truck.

"You're strong," Laney called. "I'm going to be strong one day too." Laney pumped her arms to show her biceps.

Mark laughed and said, "Hey, I got a good joke for you, Laney. What's red and white and red and white and red and white?"

Laney tilted her head, considering. "A candy cane?"

"That's one answer, but I'm thinking of something else," Mark said, grabbing hold of the end of the garbage truck once again. The truck began to move.

"Tell me!" yelled Laney at the retreating truck.

Mark bellowed the answer. "Santa Claus rolling down a hill!"

Laney giggled and waved as Mark saluted her from the back of the garbage truck.

Down the avenue they went. They passed by Harlem Coffee with their long line of bleary-eyed customers, A to Z Deli, which was just opening up, then the library, still closed for another few hours. Once they passed the library, the sisters made a right at 137th Street. They smelled the delicious, buttery sweet bread smells from Castleman's Bakery before they saw the storefront.

Castleman's Bakery, home of the legendary cheese croissants, was right across from the entrance to City College. It had sat in that same location for decades and had a loyal following of people who would cross boroughs and state lines to buy bread and pastries there. The Vanderbeeker kids truly believed the Beiderman would take one bite of the buttery-but-not-greasy, flaky-but-not-crumbly pastry and be won over at once.

Mr. Castleman was the renowned neighborhood baker, and his wife managed the front of the store. They had a son, Benny, an eighth-grader at the twins' middle school and a close friend of Isa's. He worked as a cashier at the bakery on the weekends and some days after school. At his suggestion, his parents had recently purchased an electronic touchscreen register that had all the prices programmed in, along with a credit card machine, allowing customers to sign their name with their finger. Benny, however, was the only one who knew how to operate this register. Mrs. Castleman preferred to use the antique cash register that made a brisk *ka-ching!* sound whenever the drawer opened.

"Hey hey, what's up, Vanderbeekers!" Benny called from behind the two registers with a wide grin. He wore a football jersey and blue jeans under his work apron. Jessie smiled at him, and Laney ducked under the counter and wrapped her arms around his waist.

"Hello, Princess Laney," Benny said as Laney adjusted the crown on her head.

"I have a joke for you," Laney said.

"Tell me."

"Okay, what is Santa Claus rolling down a hill? Wait. That's not it. I forgot." Laney's eyebrows were furrowed with confusion.

"What's red and white and . . ." Jessie prompted.

"Oh yeah. What's red and white and red and white and red and white?"

Benny tapped his chin with his index finger. "Hmm . . . that's a tough one. Hmm . . ."

Laney was gleeful. "Do you give up? Should I tell you?"

"Tell me. I can't think of anything."

"Santa Claus rolling down a hill!"

Benny chuckled. "Oh man, that *is* a good joke. I'm going to remember that one." Benny picked Laney up and sat her on the counter next to the register, then plucked a jam cookie from a wide-mouthed glass jar and handed it to her. Then he reached in again and retrieved one for Jessie, presenting it to her with a gallant bow.

"Thanks, Benny," Jessie said, taking a bite of the crumbly cookie. She had known him for so long that she forgot to call him Benjamin, the name he decided he wanted to be called the day he turned ten.

Mrs. Castleman peered through round tortoiseshell spectacles over the glass case containing the breads and pastries, her gaze just barely skimming the top.

"The usual, yes?" she asked.

Jessie nodded. "Also, I need three of your best breakfast goodies for our upstairs neighbor."

"How are Miss Josie and Mr. Jeet doing?" asked Mrs. Castleman.

"They're doing fine, but the pastries aren't for them. This time it's for our upstairs, upstairs neighbor. Mr. Beiderman."

Mrs. Castleman raised an eyebrow in surprise. "Mr. Beiderman?"

"He lives on the third floor. We're trying to persuade him to like us." Jessie rummaged through her bag for her wallet.

"Mr. Beiderman," Mrs. Castleman repeated softly while she leaned down to pluck pastries from the display case.

Something in the way Mrs. Castleman said his name made Jessie stop. She bent down to peer through the glass case, but she could only see Mrs. Castleman's hand reaching out to retrieve the pastries. "Do you know him, Mrs. Castleman?"

A pause. Jessie was about to ask yet again, louder, when Benny interrupted.

"So, Jessie. Did you hear about the eighth grade dance?" he asked casually, leaning his elbows on the counter. Laney still sat next to the register picking through the coins in the little cup that said "Take a penny, leave a penny."

Jessie glanced at Mrs. Castleman once more before turning back to Benny. "No. What about it?" Jessie said to Benny as she dug through her tote. Battered science notebook. A couple of pieces of candy in tired wrappers. Scuffed calculator. Oh, there was her wallet.

"Well," Benny continued, "do you think your sister would want to go?"

Jessie lifted her eyes to his. "What sister?"

Benny stuck his hands deep into the pockets of his jeans. "*Isa.* Your twin sister?"

"Isa? Go to an eighth grade dance? Benny, she's a seventh-grader. She can't go to an eighth grade dance."

"She can go *with* an eighth-grader. Which I am. An eighth-grader. And I would ask her nicely, of course. Do you think she would say yes?" Benny began to shift from foot to foot.

Laney interrupted. "I like to dance," she informed him while handing him two pennies from the "Take a penny" cup. Benny took the pennies from her and dropped them back into the cup.

Meanwhile, Jessie's mind spun like the centrifuge she'd used in science class last month. Benny wanted to take her sister to a dance? Without her? They had never gone to a school dance without each other. They had never gone to a dance with a date, ever. That would surely violate the Rule of the Twins. Somewhere in that unwritten contract, there must be a clause that clearly stated that neither was to attend a dance without the other, especially with a *date*.

"I am positive she wouldn't want to go with you, Benny. I'm sorry," Jessie said. "Not that you aren't great . . . it's just that I definitely think no."

Benny's face fell. "Why not?"

Jessie started to feel a little bad for him. "It's nothing against you. I just can't imagine her saying yes." She opened her wallet and pulled out some money.

"I like to dance," Laney repeated as she took another penny from the cup and tried to scrub it clean with the hem of her jacket.

Benny didn't respond to either sister. He carefully

rang up Jessie's order on the cash register, took her money, then handed her the change.

"Thanks, Benny," Jessie said, grabbing the bags of croissants and the goodies for Mr. Beiderman. Benny lifted Laney down from the counter and she ducked back under and took Jessie's hand.

"See you around," said Jessie with a brief wave. "Bye, Mrs. Castleman."

The two sisters left the bakery while Benny and his mother watched them disappear from view. Mrs. Castleman wisely stepped into the back room, where her husband was twisting and kneading bread, leaving her son alone with his thoughts.

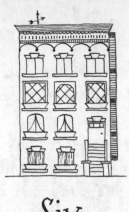

Six

The moment Jessie left the bakery, all thoughts of dances and Benny and the Rule of the Twins vanished. Laney, who carried the Beezerman's bag of pastries, surreptitiously peeked into the brown bag while they were walking home. The sugary, spicy smell of the apple turnover almost made her dizzy. She wondered if the Beezerman would mind if she took that one for herself.

"Don't even think about it," Jessie said, reaching down to cup Laney's chin. Laney puffed out her cheeks and rolled the top of the bag closed.

Isa, Hyacinth, and Oliver were waiting in the kitchen when Jessie and Laney returned home.

"Quick—we sent Mama and Papa upstairs and told them we would bring them breakfast in bed. They looked so pleased they didn't even ask any questions!" said Isa, her face flushed.

Hyacinth had taken out her special tea tray and tea things to use for the Beiderman's breakfast. The tray was faded but still pretty, with a big rainbow in the middle and three cherubs with harps floating above it. Her china teapot only had two chips, and she had folded a piece of red checkered fabric for a napkin and laid it on the side of the tray.

The kids transferred the remains from the morning's coffeepot into the teapot; then Oliver dumped three generous spoonfuls of sugar into it and Isa added milk. After Jessie stirred it, Isa placed the teapot on the tray, and Hyacinth artfully arranged the pastries from Laney's bag. To their knowledge, the Beiderman had never experienced the joy of breakfast in bed, and they were certain that Oliver's excellent idea would win him over.

"Ready?" Jessie asked Laney.

"Ready, ready!" Laney chirruped.

The Vanderbeekers went upstairs, crept past Mama and Papa's bedroom, then opened the door that led to the first-floor hallway.

"Be careful," Isa whispered.

"Break a leg," Oliver whispered.

Hyacinth didn't say anything; she just bit her lip and looked worried. They watched as Jessie and Laney went up the stairs.

The scent of laundry soap, old books, and double chocolate pecan cookies from the Vanderbeekers' floor gave way to the smell of Miss Josie's Southern Rose perfume on the second floor. The stairs leading to the third floor groaned all the way up, and the air turned musty and stale, as if the brownstone were warning them away.

Jessie took a deep breath and prepared to knock. Before she could exhale, Laney pounded her two fists on the door.

"Laney!" Jessie tried to balance the tray while preventing Laney from attacking the door again. The teapot shivered and slid to the edge of the tray. Jessie lifted up a knee to prop up the tray but overcompensated.

"Fudge!" Jessie blurted out as the teapot slid to the other side of the tray, tipped off the side, and shattered on the ground. The three pastries fell on top of it.

"Fudge, fudge, *fudge!*"

Jessie cast a look at the door. The peephole was a collection of circles getting smaller and smaller, converging on a dark round circle in the middle. Then—the circle blinked.

"Oh *fudge!*" This time Jessie's expletive was quite a bit louder. She scooped Laney up and crashed down the stairs, the destroyed breakfast left abandoned outside the Beiderman's door.

❖   ❖   ❖

Isa, Hyacinth, and Oliver were waiting by the first-floor doorway when they heard Jessie's yelling, followed by a terrific crash. Seconds later, they saw Jessie and Laney barreling down the stairs. When Isa saw the terror on Jessie's face, she did not stop to ask questions. Isa swung open the door to their apartment, and together the five Vanderbeekers scrambled inside and let the door slam behind them.

"Complete . . . fail . . ." Jessie wheezed, her back against the hallway wall.

"Shhh!" said Isa, pointing a finger at Mama and Papa's room. The kids tiptoed to Isa and Jessie's room and shut the door.

"What happened?" asked Isa the moment the door closed.

Jessie was frantic. "I lost control of the tray and everything fell. I'm sorry, Hyacinth, I broke your teapot."

Hyacinth looked back at Jessie with wide eyes.

"After I dropped the breakfast, I looked up at the door and I saw his evil eye blink at me through the peephole and it was like he was cursing me with a thousand curses! I didn't think—I should have stayed there and cleaned up or tried to explain to him or something! I'm sorry, I screwed up," Jessie babbled.

"Okay, okay, it's okay. I'll clean it up, don't worry," Isa said, pulling Jessie into a hug.

"I'll help," Hyacinth said.

"Me too," Oliver offered.

Laney was put in charge of soothing Jessie's wounded soul by feeding her cheese croissants while Isa, Hyacinth, and Oliver gathered cleaning supplies and a garbage bag and went upstairs. Tears dripped from Hyacinth's eyes as she gathered the remains of her beloved teapot and put them in the garbage bag. Oliver mopped up the spill with paper towels and mourned the ruined, soggy pastries. Isa did a final mop to get rid of the stickiness, careful to keep her eyes averted from the peephole. They slinked down the stairs, each one thinking that this was a huge setback to Operation Beiderman.

❁ ❁ ❁

While Isa, Oliver, and Hyacinth were cleaning up, Jessie and Laney delivered croissants to their parents. Laney went over to Papa's side of the bed and snuggled next to him as he scrolled through his phone reviewing job tickets, which Laney knew meant all the computer problems people wanted Papa to fix, like when someone spilled coffee on their keyboard or when the computer showed only a black screen no matter how many buttons you pushed.

Mama looked up from her own phone when Jessie stood by her bed. Mama had been clicking through a Realtor website.

"Everything okay?" Mama asked, setting her phone on the bedside table.

Jessie shrugged and handed over the bag of croissants.

"Talk to me," her mom said, beckoning Jessie to sit on the bed.

Jessie perched on the side. "This whole moving thing sucks big-time."

Mama nodded and wrapped an arm around her. "This place has so many memories." Mama looked at the wall where six years ago an unsupervised three-year-old Oliver had drawn a post-impressionist-Picasso-like depiction of their family. The miraculous thing about the artwork was that Oliver had drawn not just himself, Jessie with her signature wild-scientist hair, Isa with her typical smooth pony-tail, and his parents, but also yet-to-be-born Hyacinth and Laney.

"I feel like we need to cut out that part of the wall and bring it with us to our new home," Mama said.

"Uncle Arthur could do it," Jessie suggested.

"I don't think the Beiderman—I mean, *Mr. Beiderman*—would appreciate us gouging a hole in his wall." Mama continued to look at the drawing. Then, to Jessie's horror, she saw a tear roll down Mama's face.

"Oh, Mama, don't cry!" Jessie said, even as she felt the burning of her own eyes.

"Sweetie, don't worry about me." Mama brushed her tear away and gave Jessie a brave smile. "Just being sentimental."

Jessie's throat constricted. She wanted to rewind the last hour and do it all over again. In her mind she saw herself handling the tray with elegance and poise, presenting it to a grateful Beiderman, who accepted it with a smile. He would be so relieved to have real food after all those years of frozen dinners. With his first bite of cheese croissant his eyes would light up and he would announce that the Vanderbeekers could stay in their apartment forever.

If only the reimagined story could be reality.

Seven

The mood was somber by the time the five Vander-beeker kids gathered back downstairs to eat their own breakfast. Hyacinth felt responsible for the failed out-reach as she watched Jessie mope; after all, Jessie had wanted Hyacinth to do the first Beiderman mission. Now Hyacinth needed to fix it.

Directly after breakfast, Hyacinth retreated to her room with Franz. While her dog occupied himself by staring out the window at a bird, Hyacinth took out sewing supplies and sheets of red and green felt. Care-fully, she cut out letters spelling the Beiderman's name from the green felt; then she threaded her needle and sewed the letters onto the rectangular red piece.

The letters did not end up going across the placemat in a straight line. Instead, four letters in, she realized that there was a distinct upward slant. She tried to correct it with the next few letters, but when she reached the *M*, the name was tilting the opposite direction. By the time she finished, the name had a decidedly bumpy look about it. And something else seemed off. She thought that the *I* was before the *E*, but after she sewed the letters on, it looked a little wrong.

Hyacinth's hand was aching by the time she finished. She rolled the placemat up and tied a green velvet ribbon around it. She let her eyes linger on the green ribbon, already mourning the loss of that piece from her collection. It was not easy to part with her beautiful things.

"You ready to be brave, Franz?" asked Hyacinth. Franz lifted his front legs and rested them against her stomach.

It was time for Hyacinth to be more than just the fourth Vanderbeeker, the shy one, the scared one.

She needed to be Hyacinth the Brave: a Girl on a Mission to Save Her Home.

Together Hyacinth the Brave and Franz left their apartment and marched upstairs. The brownstone stairs whimpered all the way up.

"Be brave, be brave, be brave," Hyacinth whispered to herself. She looked down at Franz, and her faithful dog grinned at her and wagged his tail. Hyacinth squared her shoulders and knocked on the door.

The second Hyacinth knocked, she knew something bad was going to happen. She knew before she heard the stomping from inside the third-floor apartment and the barrage of clicks and bangs from locks being disengaged. She knew even before the door swung open.

Hyacinth trembled as she stood before a monster of a man with shaggy dark hair and a beard streaked with white. His face was creased and pale and lifeless. He was wearing black, black, black.

"*Leave me alone.*" His voice shocked Hyacinth. It sounded like he was talking around a mouthful of nails. "Move out of here, and *let me be.*"

Hyacinth stood frozen for a full second. No longer was she Hyacinth the Brave. She was back to being the fourth Vanderbeeker, first-class worrier and the shyest kid on 141st Street. She dropped the placemat at his feet and stumbled down the stairs, Franz at her heels. She reached the door to their apartment and slammed the door behind her.

When she reached the safety of her top bunk, she burst into tears. Big, hiccupping, drowning tears.

❋ ❋ ❋

Oliver's stomach was rumbling when he heard the door down the hall from his bedroom slam and then his little sisters' bedroom door open and shut. For a millisecond he wondered if everything was okay. When he didn't hear anything else, he put his book aside and decided to search the kitchen to see if he could find where his mom was hiding the double chocolate pecan cookies. He opened his bedroom door.

Oliver heard sobbing.

It sounded like Hyacinth.

He tried to ignore it—the cookies were calling him—but then the sobbing intensified.

Oliver knocked on Hyacinth and Laney's bedroom door. There was no answer. He opened the door and peeked inside. Franz sat on the carpet, whimpering. Hyacinth lay on her top bunk, her stuffed penguin held close to her chest.

Oliver let himself in and closed the door behind him. "Can I come up?"

There was no answer except suppressed sobs, so Oliver took that as a yes and climbed to the top bunk. Hyacinth was a sad sight, with her blotchy face and swollen eyes.

"Everything okay?" Oliver asked.

No answer.

He tried again. "Want to tell me what's wrong?"

Nothing.

"Do I need to get my sword and take someone down?"

Hyacinth sobbed out something through her tears that sounded like *miss beebee mania*, which Oliver was certain could not be correct. He gingerly patted Hyacinth's back and waited for her to be more coherent.

"I felt"—*hiccup*—"like I needed to fix"—*sob*—"what happened this morning"—*sniffle*—"with break-fast. Well, I spent *hours* making him"—*hiccup*—"a placemat, and then I brought it upstairs to him and"—*sniff*—"I thought I was Hyacinth the Brave but"—*sob*—"he was the scariest man I've ever seen." Hyacinth's eyes brimmed with fresh tears.

Oliver scowled, then rolled his shoulders and neck. "I'm going to challenge him to a pirate duel." Oliver demonstrated his hand-swipe technique. "Take that, Beiderman!"

Hyacinth looked at Oliver with watery eyes.

"After I defeat him with my superior pirate skills, we could let Franz loose and have him pee all over his door again. Would that make you feel better?"

Franz's tail thumped once against the carpet.

"I don't know why he hates us so much," Hyacinth said with a wail.

Oliver deflated. "Maybe it's best that we move. At least we'll get away from him."

Hyacinth shook her head sadly. "I love it here. I want things to go back to how they were before. Before we had to be nice to *him*." Her eyes began to well up.

Oliver, alarmed by the prospect of Hyacinth crying again, suggested that they go downstairs so she could show him her collection of buttons. It was an activity that never failed to cheer her up, even though it bored Oliver to no end. As they went down the stairs to the living room, Oliver remembered something.

"Hey, Hyacinth?"

"Yeah?"

"What did the Beiderman look like, anyway?"

Hyacinth paused to think. "Do you remember the movie Uncle Arthur took us to last year? The one where the werewolf creeps out of the cave to attack the unicorn?"

"Yeah?"

"The Beiderman looked like the werewolf."

"Wow," Oliver said as he let out the breath he didn't know he was holding. "Cool."

☀ ☀ ☀

While Oliver was trying to make Hyacinth feel better, Laney received permission from Mama to bring Paganini the bunny upstairs to Miss Josie and Mr. Jeet's place. Laney loved visiting them for many reasons:

#1. Miss Josie made the best jam cookies, with plenty of strawberry jam in the middle, and she never, ever used orange marmalade.

#2. Mr. Jeet always knew what she was saying. He didn't do that awful grownup thing where he looked at her parents or siblings to translate what she had said.

#3. Miss Josie was a terrific dancer, and she was teaching Laney how to lindy hop.

#4. Going into their apartment was like entering an enchanted garden. And Miss Josie let Laney pick flowers anytime she wanted.

Mama and Papa had told Laney that Mr. Jeet had had a stroke two years ago, which meant that he sounded and looked a little different than he used to. But that never bothered Laney; he had always been the same to her, and she loved the way he talked nice and slow so she could understand all the words. Isa and Jessie and Oliver told stories about how Mr. Jeet used to give them endless piggyback rides. He would play horsie and sleeping bear and friendly dragon.

Laney didn't remember that, but it didn't matter. Mr. Jeet was perfect in every way.

Laney lured Paganini into his carrier with a few bits of carrot, then took her time climbing up to the second floor. A few months earlier, she had stumbled going up the stairs and almost fell on Paganini and squashed him, and Laney did not want *that* to happen again. She made it upstairs without tripping, set the carrier down, and attempted many unsuccessful jumps to reach the doorbell. By her fifth jump, the door swung open and a smiling Miss Josie appeared. Miss Josie had curlers in her hair and fuzzy slippers on her feet. She greeted Laney with a big hug.

"Hello, my beautiful Laney. Come in and have some tea and cookies with Mr. Jeet and me."

Laney brushed past a large fern and skipped over to Mr. Jeet and climbed into his lap. Mr. Jeet was immaculately dressed in a pressed button-down shirt and crisp black trousers. A large daisy was stuck into his shirt pocket, and a purple bow tie with very thin white stripes lay against his throat.

"Your bow tie is very nice," Laney commented, followed by, "Does the Beiderman like cheese croissants?"

"Cheese—croissants?" Mr. Jeet repeated as he removed the daisy from his pocket and handed it to Laney. "I—don't—know." He looked at Miss Josie.

"Did you ever meet him?" pressed Laney. She took a deep whiff of the daisy before sticking it behind her ear.

Miss Josie looked uncomfortable. "I knew him back before . . . Well, never mind that. I remember he used to listen to a lot of music. He had a record player, like us. He loved jazz music."

"I like jazz music," said Laney.

Miss Josie leaned down and kissed Laney's forehead. "Me too," she said.

Mr. Jeet tugged on one of Laney's braids. "Is—Paganini—with—you?"

"He's here!" Laney slid off Mr. Jeet's lap and got the carrier. She unzipped it and the tip of Paganini's nose emerged. Miss Josie gave Mr. Jeet a sprig of cilantro, and Paganini's rabbit nose led the way over to the delicious herb, where he plucked it from Mr. Jeet's hands and ate it with both efficiency and speed. Mr. Jeet grinned, his smile lopsided.

"You—should—train—him," Mr. Jeet said. "Do—tricks."

Laney giggled. "Paganini, do tricks! That's so funny, Mr. Jeet!"

Mr. Jeet looked at her with his serious face. "Would—be—fun."

Laney realized that Mr. Jeet was not joking. She imagined her family looking at her in amazement when they saw Paganini do tricks. Then she added a spotlight and a stage and lots of clapping to her imagination.

Laney looked at Mr. Jeet with more interest. "What kind of tricks?"

Mr. Jeet pulled out another sprig of cilantro and said, "Paganini—COME." The bunny was busy rooting around in a corner behind a ficus plant and paid Mr. Jeet no attention. Mr. Jeet gestured to Laney, and she walked across the room and picked up Paganini and turned him around. Mr. Jeet repeated the command, waving the cilantro. Paganini hopped over right away at the smell of the cilantro and gobbled it up, his back molars crunching away happily.

And so the training began. Mr. Jeet instructed Miss Josie to chop a carrot into little bits. These would serve as Paganini's training tools. Together Mr. Jeet and Laney worked on "COME," rewarding Paganini with one small piece of carrot every time he successfully completed the command. It was decided that Laney would visit with Paganini every day for training. Big plans were made for a bunny show after Christmas Eve dinner.

"Can I wear a sparkly dress?" asked Laney. "And shoes with heels that tap like Mama's shoes?"

Mr. Jeet nodded. "Paganini—can—wear—a—bow—tie. I'll—lend—him—one."

As Laney put Paganini back in the carrier, she turned to Miss Josie and Mr. Jeet. "Did you know we're moving?" she asked.

Miss Josie went silent and Mr. Jeet looked away. "We know," Miss Josie finally said. "Your papa told us."

"I don't want to move. Will you still live upstairs?"

"Sweetie, I don't think we can move with you," Miss Josie replied. "We're too old to make a big move like that."

"I have an idea. I can help you move. I can carry things downstairs," Laney suggested.

"How about we see what happens. But if we can't come with you, we'll visit you, and you can visit us." Miss Josie's voice wobbled, and Mr. Jeet's head bowed lower, tears rolling down his cheeks and splashing onto his pants.

Miss Josie walked Laney and Paganini to the door and watched them descend the staircase to the first floor and safely enter their apartment. Miss Josie closed her own door, then went to her husband and kissed his head.

"It'll be okay. We'll be okay," she whispered to him, even as her own tears betrayed her.

Eight

After a lunch of grab-whatever-you-can-from-the-fridge followed by an hour of reading a massive science encyclopedia she had dragged home from the library, Jessie needed a break. She took the stairs two at a time to the bedroom in search of Isa. When she opened the door, she found Allegra, their friend from school, standing in the middle of the room wearing a frightful dress that made her look like a giant boysenberry. A bunch of other equally hideous garments were laid out on Isa's bed.

Jessie shielded her eyes and grimaced. "I'm blind! Too . . . much . . . tulle . . . disguised . . . as . . . clothes . . ."

Allegra harrumphed. "Jess, get a grip. It's not like I'm going to wear this when I walk the dog." Allegra gave a regal spin that looked like a move she learned from a terrible girly-girl movie. "This is what you wear for an eighth grade semiformal dance."

"I think Allegra looks lovely," Isa said, gazing at Allegra reverently. "Isn't that amazing that she's going to the eighth grade dance?"

Jessie grunted. "I guess." She slumped into the bean-bag chair.

Allegra looked thoughtfully at Jessie. "Jess, listen up. You could look *so* gorgeous if you wore something other than those old jeans and sweatshirts. I bet if you dressed a little nicer, and maybe used some Farewell Frizz Spray or something to smooth down your hair, an eighth-grader would invite you to the dance too."

Jessie rolled her eyes to the ceiling. "And that, my friend, is why I'm *not* going to dress differently. Eighth grade boys think they're so cool. A dance sounds like torture." Jessie looked at Isa for affirmation, but her sister wasn't paying attention.

Isa fingered one of the dresses on the bed. "Hey, can I try this one?" She held up the least abominable of the dresses, a floor-length sleeveless peach-colored dress that had a high waist and fell in soft folds to the ground.

"Sure," Allegra said. "Jess, feel free to try anything on. That sparkly blue one would look so awesome on you."

"Never going to happen," Jessie replied as she picked at her cuticles. The sparkly blue dress looked like something a six-year-old would wear to an ice-skating competition.

"Jess, help me," Isa said. Jessie got up and helped Isa gently pull the dress down over her head. Jessie smoothed the long skirt and zipped up the back. Isa turned around.

"Wow," Jessie breathed. "You look like a queen. An awesome, kick-butt queen."

Allegra clasped her hands to her chest. "That dress is *ahh-mazing* on you!" she squealed. "I *so* wish you could go to the dance too."

Jessie suddenly remembered Benny and their conversation earlier that day. Did Isa *want* to go to the dance? Generally the twins were in agreement about these types of things. But there Isa was, standing before her, looking so elegant and grown up in the peach gown, not looking a bit appalled by the idea of going to a fancy-pants dance. What had happened? Jessie had meant to mention the thing with Benny from that morning so they could both have a good laugh about it, but now she wasn't sure if Isa would think it was funny. If Isa went to this dance without her—and with a *boy*—what would it mean? It would be the first major life event they didn't experience together.

"Isa, seriously," Jessie said, a little bit louder than she meant to. "We have bigger things to worry about than dances."

"Yeah," said Isa dreamily, admiring herself from different angles in the mirror, her impeccable posture making her look stage-ready for Carnegie Hall.

"Hello!" Jessie said, waving her hands in front of Isa's face. "Moving? The Beiderman?"

"Whoa," said Allegra. "Who's moving? What Beiderman?"

Isa snapped out of her reverie and looked at Allegra.

"*We're* moving. The Beiderman is our landlord, and he isn't renewing our lease."

"We figure we have until Christmas to convince him to let us stay," Jessie added.

"But that's only four days away!" Allegra exclaimed. "What's your landlord's deal, anyway?"

Jessie shrugged. "He can't take all our noise. Or something."

Allegra planted her hands on her hips. "We need to stop him. Your brownstone is the only reason I don't run away from home and find new parents." Allegra's parents were both pediatricians and spent so much time fixing the health problems of other people's kids that Allegra believed they'd forgotten they had a daughter of their own.

"We tried to make contact with the Beiderman this morning. Did not go well," Jessie said, then filled Allegra in on the failed breakfast attempt.

"Here's what's going to happen," Allegra declared. "You're going to save your home, and here's how."

Jessie clamped her mouth shut as Allegra rattled off

a number of unreasonable ideas (including one particularly ridiculous suggestion to purchase the whole brownstone—in cash—from the Beiderman), and when Allegra ran out of ideas she talked *again* about the dance and how amazing Isa looked in the gown. Jessie didn't trust herself to join the conversation, so she slipped out the door without saying anything at all.

❖ ❖ ❖

Oliver spent a dreadfully boring twenty-three minutes looking through Hyacinth's button collection. When he left his sister peaceful and preoccupied with a craft project (most likely *another* Christmas gift), he was reminded yet again that he had not figured out Christmas presents. He didn't know how Hyacinth did it. Just two weeks ago she had made him some type of arm-warmer contraption. She was like a workaholic elf.

Oliver headed up to his bedroom to think about gifts, but when he saw his copy of *Treasure Island* sitting on his desk he had a flash of inspiration to avenge Hyacinth's honor. He pulled out a fresh sheet of notebook paper, briefly contemplated the content of his letter, then wrote the following:

To the scoundrel on the third floor,

I hope your conscience has robbed you of sleep. Being mean will earn you a black spot, and you know what that means. Be nice, or watch out. Woe be to the man who does not heed my advice.

Signed,
Your Greatest Foe

There, Oliver thought. *Short and to the point.* He was particularly proud of the part about the black spot. In *Treasure Island,* the black spot meant you were guilty of something and would be fully punished. He thought that lent a certain drama to the letter. He folded the letter into thirds, then slipped it into an envelope. He knew he should be trying to win over the Beiderman, but how would the upstairs neighbor even know that it was him writing the note anyway? It could be anyone. Oliver had really good handwriting for a nine-year-old.

He cut out letters from his *Amazing Outdoor Adventures* magazine to spell MR. BEIDERMAN, then pasted them onto an envelope, laying them out like the ransom notes he always imagined getting if someone were to steal Franz or Paganini. That would strike fear into the Beiderman's heart, he was sure of it.

For the third time that day, a Vanderbeeker kid climbed the stairs to the top floor. Oliver stealthily slipped the letter under the door, then snuck back down the stairs, quiet as a mouse. *Oh yeah, who is the man?* Let it be known that he, Oliver S. Vanderbeeker, was not to be pushed around when it came to his family.

When Oliver reentered his apartment, feeling as smug as a peacock with a full plume of feathers, he ran straight into Jessie.

"Do you think I need to dress differently?" Jessie demanded.

Oliver winced. This could not end well.

"No," said Oliver with complete honesty, hoping that was the right answer.

"Why not?" Jessie asked him belligerently. "Don't you think my old jeans and stained sweatshirts are gross? Don't you think I should dress nicer?"

Oliver decided to change tactics. "Um . . . yes? Maybe you should get nicer clothes?"

"So you think I'm a big loser too, huh? You and everyone else," Jessie snapped.

"Why don't you tell me what you want me to say so I can say it and go on with my life," Oliver shot back.

"Sorry." Jessie didn't look or sound sorry.

"Well, go eat some ice cream or get a chocolate croissant from Castleman's or something."

Jessie's eyes flashed. Apparently that was yet *another* wrong thing for Oliver to say, although he couldn't imagine why. Chocolate always cheered up his sisters. Oliver inched against the hallway wall, trying to give Jessie as much space as possible.

"Listen, I'm an innocent bystander here," Oliver entreated, hands held up in surrender. He disappeared into his bedroom and shut the door. Two seconds later, he opened the door just wide enough for his hand to sneak out and hang a "Don't Bother the Beast" sign on his doorknob before closing it soundly again.

Jessie stared at Oliver's door and the ridiculous sign hanging from the doorknob. She sighed. She really did want a chocolate croissant—maybe two—but she *did not* want to go back to Castleman's. She wanted to lie in bed under the covers and feel miserable about life.

Jessie's bedroom door opened, and Isa and Allegra emerged, back in their regular clothes. Jessie sighed with relief and took a few deep, calming breaths. Now they could go back to concentrating on what really mattered, like saving their home.

"Jess, we're going to Castleman's for a croissant. Come with us," said Isa.

"NO!" Jessie yelled, her heart rate kicking up. "I mean, yes. I mean, NO. I mean, don't you think we should be brainstorming more about the Beiderman?"

"We're just running out for a few minutes. You're the one who always quotes that scientific study about how the chemicals in chocolate help the mind work," Isa pointed out. "Besides, I want to talk to Benny."

Jessie's stomach dropped. She could not, absolutely

could not, go back to Castleman's today after what had happened that morning with Benny. Especially since she hadn't told Isa that Benny wanted to ask her to the dance. Especially since it now seemed that Isa *did* want to go to the dance. Especially since Jessie did not want Isa to go to the dance.

"I've got a headache. And I have my science fair research to do. And I need to do some sit-ups. You know, keep the body fit." *Stop talking, stop talking, stop talking,* Jessie demanded of herself.

"Jess, is everything . . . all right?" Isa's brow furrowed in confusion.

Jessie nodded. She didn't trust herself to speak anymore.

"We'll be right back. Then we can think more about the Beiderman. We'll get you a chocolate croissant." Isa and Allegra stepped away from Jessie, Isa still eyeing her sister critically. Jessie attempted to smile, which only made Isa look more concerned. Jessie scooted into their bedroom and shut the door. She dropped down onto her bed, covered her head with a pillow, and let out a low, tortured groan.

Nine

"That was weird," Allegra said to Isa once they were outside and on their way to Castleman's Bakery.

"I think this moving stuff is making her nuts." Her sister was not taking the news about moving well. Isa had to come up with a new plan to conquer the Beiderman once and for all, and she had to do it fast.

Allegra shrugged and returned to her new favorite topic, the eighth grade dance. "My mom said Carlson will bring me a corsage and I should get him a boutonniere. Isn't that wild? I think corsages are so gorgeous. How do you think I should wear my hair? Should I leave it down? I wonder if Carlson is going to wear a suit. Wouldn't that be so romantic? I'm so excited. Do you want me to ask Carlson whether he knows anyone who would take you? You're so pretty, I know it wouldn't be hard to find someone. I wish I had your big brown eyes and long eyelashes. How about that boy who sits next to you in orchestra? What's his name? Henry? I love his red hair. And those freckles! So cute."

Isa nodded halfheartedly. She was glad to be going to Castleman's; she wanted to tell Benny about the move and ask his advice about the Beiderman. Allegra was great, but when Isa talked to Benny she felt like he stopped everything he was doing and really, truly *listened* to her.

They turned the corner and made their way down the street and into the bakery. When they entered, Benny was alone at the counter.

"Hey, Benjamin," Allegra called out, walking in first. Benny gave a wave. When Isa stepped in, he frowned at her. But that couldn't be right. Benny had never *not* smiled when he saw her.

"Hi, Benny," Isa said. She smiled at him, but he was definitely frowning. "Everything okay?"

"Yup," Benny replied, not sounding like anything was okay at all. "What do you want?"

Isa stilled. "Oh. Okay. Um...two chocolate croissants," Isa said, trying to keep her voice steady. "Wait, change that to three. I want to bring one back to Jessie."

Benny's frown turned into a full-blown scowl and his eyes narrowed. He pulled out a piece of wax paper and used it to grab three chocolate croissants from the glass case. He dropped them into a white bag and thrust it at her.

"Anything else?" he asked.

Isa shook her head, taking the bag as if it were filled with snakes. She handed him the money and waited as he made change. He dropped some quarters in her hand and focused his attention on a point just beyond her left ear, where a picture of a grazing dairy cow hung on the wall.

"Benny," Isa began, clutching the bag tighter. "I wanted to tell you—"

"Isa, don't worry about it, okay?" Benny said, still avoiding her gaze. "It's not a big deal."

"Wait a second. You already know?" Isa said, confused.

"Yeah, I know. Jessie told me this morning."

"O-kay," Isa said slowly. "Don't you have anything to say about it?"

Benny met Isa's eyes. "What do you want me to say? It's fine. It doesn't matter."

Isa stepped back, her fingers gripping the bag so tightly her knuckles turned white. He didn't care that she was moving? "I thought you would . . . Oh, never mind." Isa swallowed. "I guess I'll see you later."

Benny shrugged and turned around, disappearing through the swinging doors that led to the back of the store. Isa stood there for a moment staring at the empty space he left behind.

"Geez," said Allegra, who had been unusually silent during the entire exchange. "What's wrong with *him*?"

Isa felt tears burning in her eyes. She didn't trust herself to respond.

※ ※ ※

Oliver and Laney stood at the bottom of the stairs watching Mama's parade of boxes pile up along the hallway. George Washington was having a terrific time jumping up on the stacks and swiping his claws through the cardboard.

Laney pointed to a word on a white box and looked at Oliver.

"That says 'DONATE,'" Oliver told her.

Mama bumped a garbage bag down the stairs.

"What's that, Mama?" Laney asked.

"Things to throw away," Mama replied, wiping her forehead with the sleeve of her sweatshirt.

"But, Mama," Oliver protested, pointing the tip of his sword at the blue T-shirt poking out the top of the bag. "That's my favorite T-shirt!"

"Sweetie, that was your favorite T-shirt two years ago. There's a weird smell to it. It's not even donate-able. Is that a word? 'Donate-able'?"

Oliver dropped his sword and pulled the shirt out. "Do not throw this away!"

Meanwhile, Laney threw the lid aside from one of the white cardboard boxes, rummaged through the box, removed a pair of old floral leggings, and stretched the waistband around her head to make a hat.

"Laney, don't you dare take anything out of that box without telling me," Mama warned. "I don't want to see everything we're donating back in your bedroom."

"Hey," said Papa, coming down the stairs with a slight swagger. He wore his coveralls and had his toolbox in one hand. "Guess what I just fixed."

"Mama wanted to throw this shirt away," Oliver said, holding it up so Papa could see.

"Of course she's not throwing that away," Papa scoffed. "You made your first free throw—all net, may I add—with that shirt on. It's got basketball mojo. Just like my coveralls have Mr. Fix-It mojo."

Papa and Oliver bumped fists, Laney grinned, and Mama rolled her eyes.

"I hope your coveralls and T-shirt have Pack-Up-the-Apartment mojo," Mama said, "because that's what I need from both of you right now."

George Washington mewled and ran his claws along the side of a box of books, and Mama turned her wrath onto the cat. "George Washington! If you touch one more box, I'm giving your dinner to the nice kittens living in the backyard!"

"Mama, look!" Laney cried from her spot by the white DONATE box. She still wore the leggings hat, and the fabric for the legs flapped around her face. "These are *records!*"

Mama collapsed on a kitchen stool and took a long drink of water. "I found those at the back of the up-

stairs closet. They may have been here from the previous tenants."

"Miss Josie can use them. She has a record player."

Mama looked defeated. "Okay, bring them upstairs
and ask Miss Josie if she wants them. There's some
jazz in there."

"Jazz!" Laney exclaimed. She grabbed the stack and
whispered loudly to Oliver. "Jazz! *The Beegerman*
likes jazz!" Oliver hushed her, then grabbed the records from Laney's arms and dragged her upstairs.

"How do you know the Beiderman likes jazz?" he
asked when they were out of Mama's earshot.

"Miss Josie said that long ago he used to listen to
jazz all the time," Laney answered. "Can we bring a
record up to him?"

"You're absolutely sure? Like, absolutely, *absolutely*
sure?" Oliver asked.

"I'm sure!" Laney said, bouncing up and down. Together they chose a record with a picture on the front
of a man named Duke Ellington playing the piano.

Oliver and Laney crept upstairs, hand in hand. A
sigh sounded with each step leading to the third floor,
where they left the offering at his door.

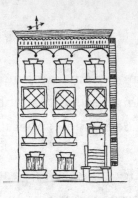

Ten

The five Vanderbeeker kids were unabashedly eavesdropping on their mother's phone conversation. They knew from her voice and her pacing back and forth across the room that something bad was going down.

"I'm sorry, Mr. Beiderman, that is not enough notice," Mama barked into her cell phone. "It's the holidays! We have boxes all over the place! There's absolutely no way."

Papa came in from the backyard, wiping his hands on his coveralls. "Hey, kids!" he boomed.

"Shhh!" responded the children, waving him away without taking their eyes off Mama.

"We're eavesdropping," Hyacinth said in a loud whisper, holding her index finger to her lips.

"Mr. Beiderman," Mama continued, her voice going up an octave, "you realize that the apartment is not going to look its best if you show it now, right?"

Pause.

"Okay. Fine. Goodbye." Mama stabbed a button on her phone and tossed it onto an end table.

The Vanderbeeker kids and Papa surrounded Mama, waiting for an explanation.

Mama massaged her temples. "Mr. Beiderman will have a real estate broker start showing the apartment to prospective renters beginning tomorrow. He *strongly* suggests that we not be in the apartment when it is shown." Mama gritted her teeth when she said *strongly*. "The broker will try to give us at least twenty-four hours' notice."

"Is that legal?" asked Papa, shocked.

"Apparently it's in our lease and we signed off on it. The landlord has the right of entry for the purpose of showing the space to a prospective tenant in the last thirty days of our lease," Mama recited in a monotone voice.

"You're kidding," Oliver said flatly, his arms crossed.

"That makes no sense!" cried Jessie. "The probability that he could rent this place out would increase significantly if the apartment were vacant." Her eyes flitted between Mama and Papa.

"Landlords can do it," Mama said, "but it would have been *nice* if he didn't. Oh, fudge, there is so much to do." Mama looked at the state of the ground floor. "Mr. Beiderman's Realtor is showing the apartment tomorrow morning at eleven."

Papa sighed. "Hon, why don't I take the kids out while you do some packing. And I'll try to talk to the Beiderman—I mean, *Mr.* Beiderman—later tonight." Mama nodded, then went up the stairs two at a time. A second later they heard her dragging more boxes around.

"Someone else is actually going to live here? In *our* home?" asked Hyacinth worriedly.

"That blows!" Oliver said. He kicked the wall, leaving black smudges on the white paint.

"Don't kick the wall," Papa said absently as he adjusted his glasses.

"Someone is going to live in *my* room?" Oliver asked. He kicked the wall again.

"They'll probably make it back into a closet," Jessie said. "That's what it was before you were born."

"But—why— My books—?" Oliver spluttered.

"You know what we need around here?" Papa said, attempting to change the anxious mood. "Some holiday spirit! Let's get a Christmas tree!"

"What's the point?" Jessie said, flopping onto a kitchen stool and burying her head in her hands. "We'll have to take it down in a few days anyway."

"Yeah," said Isa, Oliver, and Hyacinth in dejected agreement, while Laney yelled, "Tree! Tree! I want a tree!"

Everyone stared at Laney.

"And we can decorate it," Laney continued, "and put lights up, and the presents go under the tree, and I'm gonna make ornaments . . ." She started skipping around the kitchen. "And I'm gonna give Paganini a big carrot for a present, and I'm gonna wrap it . . ."

Papa looked at the older kids. "So, are we getting a tree or what?"

The older kids watched Laney run over to Paganini, lift up one floppy ear, and whisper all her grand plans for the tree.

"Okay," said Isa.

"Fine," said Oliver.

"I guess," said Jessie.

"Yeah," said Hyacinth.

Papa pulled his coveralls off. Underneath he was wearing jeans and a T-shirt that said "I'm Here Because You Broke Something." "That's the Christmas spirit, kids!"

The Vanderbeeker kids put on their winter gear and headed out the door.

"Hello, Vanderbeekers!" Angie yelled as she raced down the street on her bike. "Oliver, you owe me a basketball game!"

"You're on!" Oliver yelled back.

A window opened on the second floor of the brownstone.

"Hello, dear ones!" called out Miss Josie.

"Hello, Miss Josie!" the kids chorused. Laney blew kisses to the second floor, which were returned with equal enthusiasm.

A gentleman in baggy pants, an oversized jacket, and headphones swaggered by holding a rhinestone-studded leash attached to a pocket-sized Chihuahua.

"Yo, Vanderbeekers," he said as he fist-bumped each one.

"Yo, Big Zee," they answered.

"Did you ever notice," Isa said to Jessie after watching Big Zee stride down the street with his Chihuahua skipping behind him, "that we know everyone in this neighborhood?"

Jessie nodded. "Feels like *Sesame Street*."

"It's giving me a Beiderman idea," Isa murmured.

Jessie studied Isa, wanting to ask more, but then Oliver threw a handful of pine needles on her head and Jessie's thoughts turned solely to revenge as she chased him down the street.

It was a twenty-minute walk to the Christmas tree stand, requiring the Vanderbeekers to cross a bridge that connected Harlem to the Bronx. "It's tradition," Papa had insisted when the kids suggested they go to the Christmas tree stand around the corner rather than walking to the Bronx.

"When I was a little boy," Papa said in his reminiscing voice, "my dad took us across the bridge to Mr. Ritchie's Christmas tree stand. This was back when Christmas trees only cost five dollars," Papa added.

The kids nodded. They had heard this story so many times, Jessie could mouth the words along with Papa.

"One year, my dad broke his arm. He couldn't work for six weeks while it healed, and we had no money for a tree or presents that year. When I walked by Mr. Ritchie's Christmas tree stand one day on the way to the subway, he asked me why we hadn't gotten a tree yet. I told him about my dad's arm, and he had me choose a tree and take it home anyway. He insisted that the tree would brighten up the holiday, and he was right."

The tree stand was on a corner right next to a set of basketball courts, and when they got there, they found Mr. Ritchie sitting on a blue plastic milk crate listening to a portable radio that gave out static in far greater measure than the Tchaikovsky concerto he had it tuned to. When Mr. Ritchie saw them, he stood up and held out a hand to Papa.

"Good to see you, Mr. Ritchie," Papa said as he clapped his other hand on Mr. Ritchie's shoulder. Papa pulled a thick forest-green scarf from his backpack, and Isa helped Papa wrap it around Mr. Ritchie's neck.

"From Mrs. Vanderbeeker," Papa explained.

Mr. Ritchie fingered the end of the scarf and gave a satisfied nod and a grunt.

Laney grabbed Mr. Ritchie's hand and swung it back and forth. "I like your gold tooth," she told him. "I want one too."

Mr. Ritchie rewarded her with a small smile, his gold tooth glinting against the light of the street lamps.

"We want a tall tree," Jessie said to Mr. Ritchie, raising her arm to indicate the height. "If the tree was six feet and four inches exactly, it would fit perfectly in our living room."

"It has to be fluffy, not skinny," Oliver added, his arms splayed wide.

"We need one with a good, straight branch on the top to stick the star on," Hyacinth said.

"It has to be perfect," Isa said with a soft sigh as she fiddled with the buttons on her coat.

While her siblings made their demands, Laney had a different idea of the perfect Christmas tree. It didn't take long for her to select the most crooked, most pathetic, patchiest pine tree in the bunch. Then she coerced Papa into dragging the tree to her sisters and brother.

Laney tugged on Isa's arm to get her attention. "This

is it!" Laney declared, jabbing her finger at the tree she had chosen.

"Seriously?" asked Oliver. "You want our last Christmas tree to look like it was pulled out of a forest fire?"

"Ollie!" Laney protested, stomping her foot and pouting. "I love it! It's cute and tall and I like the branches and I want it!"

The siblings looked at each other. Mr. Ritchie watched the Vanderbeekers with his hands clasped behind him, awaiting the final decision.

Isa was the first to cave.

"Laney has never chosen the tree before," Isa admitted with an indifferent shrug.

"Yeah, for a reason," Oliver muttered.

"C'mon," Jessie protested. "We're supposed to get a tall, fluffy, *symmetrical* tree. This tree"—Oliver pointed to the offending arbor—"fulfills exactly *zero* of our specifications."

"I think it looks great," Hyacinth said loyally. After all, Laney was her roommate.

Laney's face broke into a huge grin that took up half her face, and even Oliver had to admit that it was worth getting an ugly tree for that smile.

"I guess the tree *is* sort of symbolic," Jessie admitted.

"And I want this one too," Laney said, grabbing a tiny tree that sat next to Mr. Ritchie's milk-crate stool. She thrust it at her dad while bouncing up and down.

"Give a girl an inch, she'll take a mile," murmured Oliver.

"Honey, we're not getting two trees," Papa said to Laney.

"Not for me, silly! For Miss Josie and Mr. Jeet!" Laney said.

Papa relented. Mr. Ritchie wrapped the tree in netting while Papa pulled out his wallet to pay. Laney carried the small tree, and Papa hitched the bigger one on his shoulder. The dearth of boughs and pine needles made it light and easy to carry.

The Vanderbeekers waved goodbye to Mr. Ritchie, and Papa led the way home. They left the Bronx and went back over the bridge. The sun had set behind the castle on the hill, and the lights from the city sparkled on the water. A tugboat made its way down the river, causing the water to crash into the rocks along the shorelines.

Ten minutes later, the Vanderbeekers rounded the

corner onto their sleepy street. The church with the stained-glass windows was illuminated from the inside, which gave the building an ethereal look. All down the block trees were wrapped in twinkling white lights for the holidays. Christmas trees and menorahs were displayed in the windows of many apartments.

The red brick brownstone welcomed them home with the warm glow of lamps in the ground floor, first floor, and second floor. The top floor was, as usual, hauntingly dark. Oliver opened the basement door just as Mama came down the stairs with a big box in her arms.

"Home so soon?" Mama asked.

"We got a winner," Papa replied as he screwed the tree into the holder in the living room.

Mama put down her box and inspected it. "I think you brought home the wrong tr —"

Laney interrupted. "Isn't it perfect, Mama?" she asked reverently.

"—or not," Mama finished. She crouched down next to Laney, who gazed rapturously at the bedraggled tree. Mama took a second look.

"I think it's lovely," Mama said. "Did you choose it yourself?"

"Yes, I did," Laney declared.

By this time Papa had unearthed the box of Christmas decorations from the depths of the hallway closet. The kids surrounded it, eager to see the contents that had been locked away for the past eleven months. Papa lifted the box flaps, and suddenly there were candy canes that were who knows how old, the nativity that was missing Joseph, the snowman nesting dolls, and the smooth wooden plane ornaments that had belonged to Papa as a child, which Oliver so treasured.

It quickly became apparent that this tree offered unique decorating obstacles. The lack of boughs made it difficult to hang the ornaments evenly, so the kids had to hang ten or more ornaments per branch. Isa and Jessie supervised the decorating, moving ornaments around so the larger ones hung on the back of the boughs and the smaller ones hung from the tips. Mama set out cookies, and after an hour of arranging ornaments and eating cookies and singing and reminiscing about Christmases past, the tree trimming was complete. They held their breath as Papa flipped the switch for the tree lights.

The tree was proud and majestic. The brownstone walls pulsed from the twinkling Christmas tree, making the walls look like they were breathing.

Papa saw the tree and was reminded of the many Christmas trees he had dragged into the brownstone and set up in that exact spot. He couldn't believe this would be the last Christmas they would spend here. Mama looked at the tree and remembered her children as toddlers, when they used to pull down ornaments. For many years they had only decorated the top half of the tree so the ornaments were out of reach.

Oliver looked at the tree and then at the cookie platter, noticing that only one cookie was left. He snatched it before anyone else could beat him to it. Sure, he had already eaten four, but all was fair in love and cookies. Laney looked at the tree and thought how perfect it was, the most perfect tree in the world. Hyacinth looked at the tree but didn't really see it; she was thinking about a complete stranger moving into the brownstone, into her bedroom! Isa gazed at the tree and thought about her new Beiderman idea, while Jessie looked at her sister, wondering when she should tell Isa about Benny.

Eleven

That night, when all the kids were in bed, Mama and Papa sat in the living room holding thick ceramic mugs filled with hot chocolate spiced with cayenne and cinnamon. They gazed at the twinkling tree and relaxed into the peace of the evening.

"Remember when Oliver was four and woke up early on Christmas and came downstairs and unwrapped every present under the tree looking for a train set?" Papa asked.

Mama laughed. "Jessie and Isa were so mad. I don't think I've ever seen Jessie's face that shade of red!"

"They didn't speak to him for a whole week! But I don't even think Oliver noticed. He was too busy with those trains," Papa said.

Mama sipped her hot chocolate. "I always imagined living here forever. I thought Jessie and Isa would leave for prom from here. We would take a photo of them right there." Mama pointed to a spot next to the large picture window by the front door.

Papa frowned. "Our daughters aren't allowed to date until *after* college, right?"

Mama ignored him. "I always thought the kids would spend their entire childhoods here. You know, having the same type of childhood you had. Being supported by the neighborhood. Knowing everyone by name."

"Real estate is changing," Papa said. "An apartment that holds all of us *and* has a position for a super doesn't come up anymore."

"What about rentals without a super position? Can we afford that?" Mama asked.

Papa shook his head. "I've been looking at our budget. I can't make the numbers work. The discounted rent for my superintendent duties makes a huge difference."

"I could expand my business. Make more cakes and macarons . . . or something," Mama said, her mind already working out how to manufacture more hours in her day.

Papa shook his head. "Hon, we're both working too much already."

Mama laid her head on Papa's shoulder. "I hate to bring this up, but what about Ottenville? I'm sure my parents would be thrilled about that."

There was a long pause.

"I don't know," Papa said miserably. "I've lived here all my life. Our jobs are here. What about Isa and Mr. Van Hooten? The kids and their school? Mr. Jeet and Miss Josie?" Papa stared into his mug. "It would be really hard to start all over."

"I know. But it might be our only option."

"Should we tell the kids what's going on?"

Mama hesitated before speaking. "Let's wait. Let them have a few more days of peace before we break the news." She caught herself. "*If* we have to break the news."

Mama and Papa were so engrossed in their own thoughts and conversation that they didn't hear the two sets of footsteps pitter-patter down the upstairs hallway.

"Oliver, wake up. NOW."

"Blurgh. Hrmph. Go away, whoever you are."

"It's me, Hyacinth. You have to get up. Emergency meeting."

Oliver opened one eye. Hyacinth had climbed up onto his loft bed and and her face was two inches away from his. Laney was standing on the ground with her blanket in her hand and a thumb in her mouth. Before Oliver could fully wake up, he found himself being led from his warm bed and into Jessie and Isa's room.

"Isa, wake up!" Hyacinth pried open one of her sister's eyelids.

"What the . . ." Isa batted away Hyacinth's hand and rolled toward the wall.

Jessie shot up out of bed. "What's going on? Is there a fire? Grab Isa's violin!"

"No fire, but Hyacinth says it's an emergency," Oliver said, collapsing onto the carpet and leaning against Jessie's bed. His eyelids drifted closed.

"This is so important," said Hyacinth, walking to the window and yanking aside the heavy curtains so a beam of light from the street lamp fell right across Isa's bed. "I was taking Laney to the bathroom, and we overheard Mama and Papa talking downstairs."

"Close the curtains, please," moaned Jessie.

"Wait a second." Isa rolled back toward her siblings, squinting against the harsh lamplight. "Laney wakes you up in the middle of the night when she has to go to the bathroom?"

"It's 'cause the monsters," Laney said matter-of-factly. "They have big mouths and sharp teeth and gobble me up if I go into the bathroom by myself." Laney demonstrated by opening her mouth and chomping down.

"Note to self," Jessie murmured. "Put night-light in the bathroom."

"Night-lights don't help," Hyacinth informed her.

Laney shook her head, her curls bouncing around her. "The not-nice monsters use night-lights to trick me."

"Note to self," Jessie said. "Never share a room with Laney."

Oliver had since fallen back asleep, but woke

himself up when he toppled over sideways onto the rug.

Hyacinth sighed loudly. "Does anyone want to know what Laney and I overheard?"

Jessie looked at the two sisters. Laney was not known for being a reliable interpreter of conversations. Hyacinth was slightly better, but sometimes the facts still got jumbled.

"Mama said something about prom," Laney reported. "What's a prom?"

"Suspicions confirmed. Unreliable witness," Jessie mumbled. "Prom is, like, a million years away." She lay back down on her bed and pulled the comforter over her head.

"Listen!" Hyacinth said, stomping her foot. "Mama and Papa are thinking about *not* staying in the neighborhood. We're leaving Harlem!"

Isa, Jessie, and Oliver suddenly looked more awake.

"No way," Oliver said obstinately. "Papa said we were going to stay in the neighborhood. I remember."

Hyacinth shook her head. "They said we have to move to *Ottenville*."

"What? That's crazy. *Ottenville?* That's, like, four hours away. *By car.* We don't even have a car," Jessie said.

"Cars are 'spensive," Laney notified them.

"Papa said the apartments here cost too much," Hyacinth added.

Isa crossed her arms. "How would I get to my violin lessons with Mr. Van Hooten if we lived in Ottenville?"

"You would need a new violin teacher. Someone who lives in Ottenville," Jessie said.

"Impossible," said Isa. "I can't have anyone teach me but Mr. Van Hooten."

"Will Miss Josie and Mr. Jeet come with us?" asked Laney.

"Probably not," Isa said. "They have family here in New York City. I don't think they know anyone in Ottenville."

"They'll know us," Laney said, pouting. "We're family."

"It could be worse," said Isa. "We could be going to . . . I don't know. Siberia or something."

"Jimmy L doesn't live in Ottenville. Or Siberia," Oliver said.

"Franz *hates* Ottenville," Hyacinth informed her siblings. "So many squirrels!"

"Stupid Beiderman!" exclaimed Jessie.

Oliver stood up. "We still have three days to convince him."

"That's not that much," Jessie said. "The probability of success went way down after I screwed up the last mission."

"No," Hyacinth corrected her. "*I* screwed up the last mission."

"It doesn't matter," Isa interjected. "We can still do this. I had a really great idea when we were walking to get the Christmas tree. Listen."

The kids leaned forward as Isa shared her idea. Then they stayed up for another hour, making plans late into the night while the radiators puffed warmth around them.

SUNDAY, DECEMBER 22

Twelve

Help us save our home!"

"Sign our petition! Only takes a minute!"

"Mr. Johnson, please sign our petition!"

"Hey, Miss Walker, did you hear about us having to leave our home? Want to sign our petition?"

A cold front had entered New York City the night before, and temperatures had plunged into the thirties. The Vanderbeeker kids were bundled up in their heaviest winter coats, weighed down with scarves, hats, earmuffs, and multiple pairs of socks. Jessie had dressed Laney in so many layers that Isa feared if Laney fell down she wouldn't be able to get up by herself. Together they canvassed the sidewalk outside their building on 141st Street, equipped with clip-

boards and pens. The night before, they had made
multiple copies of the following petition:

Save Our Home!

Mr. Beiderman, the landlord at the red brownstone
on 141st Street, refuses to renew the lease held by the
Vanderbeeker family. Without the Vanderbeeker family,
there would be a decline in happiness & quality of life in Harlem.

⌒⌒⌒ Don't let it happen! ⌒⌒⌒

We, the undersigned, respectfully ask that Mr. Beiderman renew the
Vanderbeeker lease indefinitely.

Name	Address	Signature

Since the Internet was disconnected, Mama and Papa had gone to the library to use the computer to look up apartment listings. They asked the kids to go to Miss Josie and Mr. Jeet's place because the real estate broker was showing the apartment that morning. It gave the Vanderbeeker kids the perfect opportunity to collect signatures for their petition while their parents were gone. Miss Josie and Mr. Jeet sat on the brownstone stoop, a fleece blanket spread over their laps, keeping an eye on things.

The kids were spaced out along the street, flagging down their neighbors and other pedestrians, explaining their plight. Each had his or her own unique approach.

"If you sign this 'tition, I'll give you a giant hug!" Laney said to anyone who passed by. (She was getting the most signatures.)

Hyacinth was a hit among people walking their dogs. She had baked a fresh batch of peanut butter dog biscuits that morning and was handing them out like Halloween candy.

Oliver had called Jimmy L earlier to round up his group of friends to support the petition. At the moment, Oliver was surrounded by his basketball buddies, who signed their own names and made up additional names and addresses to fill up the sheets.

"I think Don Old Dock is a little too obvious," Oliver said as he looked over Jimmy L's shoulder.

"Dang. I thought it was a good one." Jimmy L's voice was muffled by his scarf. He scratched out the fictitious name and wrote "Mike L. Jordan" instead.

Isa was down at the corner talking to Mrs. Castleman.

"We had no idea you were moving, dear," Mrs. Castleman said, patting Isa's shoulder with a gloved hand.

"Benny knew," Isa said, avoiding Mrs. Castleman's eyes as she twisted the pen around the string that attached it to the clipboard. "Jessie told him yesterday."

"I wonder why he didn't say anything about it," Mrs. Castleman replied. "But he *has* seemed grouchy lately." She leaned toward Isa confidentially. "You know how teenagers get. I'll tell him to come by. You always make him feel better."

Isa reached out and grabbed Mrs. Castleman's arm. "No! No, it's . . . okay. I'll stop by the bakery soon." Isa's strange visit with Benny the previous day was still bothering her. She handed Mrs. Castleman the clipboard. "Do you want to sign our petition? We're trying to convince the Beiderman to let us stay."

Mrs. Castleman abruptly dropped the clipboard and it clattered to the street.

Isa bent down to pick it up, and when she rose she saw that Mrs. Castleman's face had turned pale. "Mrs. Castleman? Is everything okay?"

"Yes, yes. Sorry. I forgot Mr. Beiderman was your landlord," Mrs. Castleman said, her hands trembling.

"You know the Beiderman—I mean, Mr. Beiderman?"

"No. Yes. Not well. I—" Mrs. Castleman pivoted and walked away from Isa.

"Mrs. Castleman?" Isa called out, but Mrs. Castleman waved her arm as if she were shooing away a bad dream. Isa watched her disappear, then crossed the street to join Jessie.

"Hey! Mr. Voulos!" Jessie called out. "Sign our petition! Hey, you! Guy in the black hat! I know you see me! What's your name? Freddy?"

When Jessie paused to blow into her hands and rub them together, Isa leaned in to her sister.

"I just saw Mrs. Castleman, and I think she knows the Beiderman," Isa whispered.

"You know, she acted really weird yesterday when I mentioned his name!" Jessie said.

Before Jessie and Isa could talk more, a new batch of neighbors came out and the twins got busy getting more signatures. When the Vanderbeeker kids had been out for about an hour, they convened back at the brownstone. Miss Josie and Mr. Jeet looked relieved to go inside.

"My bones are chilled!" Miss Josie said as she led the way to the front door. "Come on, Laney dear, let's go inside and warm up with a little visit from Paganini."

✧ ✧ ✧

Laney put on her panda jacket, collected Paganini, and grabbed the small Christmas tree before heading to the second floor. Pausing before Miss Josie and Mr. Jeet's door, she looked up at the third floor. It was very dark and very creepy up there. Laney set Paganini's carrier on the doormat, then carried the little tree upstairs. The stairs felt unsteady, as if they would collapse. Was the brownstone trying to keep her from going upstairs? Laney held the tree tighter and went up three more steps. She knew the Beezleman needed a Christmas tree more than anyone. She got up to the third floor, set the tree right in front on his doorstep, and hurried back down to the second floor and knocked on the door.

It opened immediately. "My dear Panda-Laney!" said Miss Josie after glancing at her little friend wrapped in her panda attire.

Panda-Laney stepped inside and said hi to Mr. Jeet while Miss Josie busied herself chopping carrots, pouring glasses of milk, and setting out a plate of raspberry jam cookies. Panda-Laney unzipped Paganini's bag, and the little rabbit hopped out with a flourish, gazing around for something edible, nose twitching rhythmically. Finding nothing, he made his way over to the bookcase and attempted to dig a hole through the carpet.

Mr. Jeet held a small piece of carrot in his hand. "Paganini—COME!" he commanded.

Paganini, hearing the voice of the man who gave him delicious carrots, hopped over and was rewarded by a treat and a gentle ear rub. Panda-Laney took turns giving the command, Paganini responding regardless of where Laney went in the apartment. For his final test, Panda-Laney went into Miss Josie and Mr. Jeet's bedroom, then called "Come!" Paganini zigzagged his way out of the living room, skidded on the wood floor, and found Panda-Laney with no problem.

"He did it!" Panda-Laney cried, jumping up and down and almost knocking down a vase filled with wildflowers onto the carpet. Mr. Jeet laughed with a funny *heh heh heh*.

Together Mr. Jeet and Panda-Laney worked with Paganini a few more minutes before ending their training session. After Panda-Laney said goodbye, she couldn't help peeking upstairs at the door to the Beiderman's apartment.

The Christmas tree was gone.

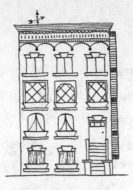

Thirteen

Oliver was in a pickle. The Christmas tree already had a substantial pile of presents under it. Not that Oliver was checking out his gifts, but he *did* notice that many of the presents bore his name, while he had not contributed anything. Now that he thought about it, wasn't it unfair that he had to give *six* presents for Christmas while Jimmy L—who did not have any brothers or sisters—only had to worry about two?

Oliver was not a good present giver. It did not matter whether he put a lot of thought into the gift or not. Actually, it seemed as though the more thought he put into something, the less the person liked it.

Oliver took his stegosaurus bank down from the

shelf. He pried open the bottom plug and shook the money out. A handful of pennies and nickels fell onto his desk. Oliver tilted the bank, stuck his fingers inside, and felt around. He pulled out two dollars but nothing else. With $2.36 laid before him on his desk, Oliver tried to think back to what he could have spent money on. He guessed he *did* buy churros almost every day after school from Manny the churro guy, who had a cart he wheeled around the neighborhood. There was something about the fried dough covered with cinnamon sugar that Oliver could not get enough of.

Oliver knew that $2.36 would not go far for Christmas presents.

Fortunately, it was almost two o'clock and time for his weekly basketball game with Jimmy L, which meant he had permission to stop thinking about presents. Oliver went downstairs, where Hyacinth was doing something with yarn and two sticks. When Hyacinth saw her brother approaching, she quickly jammed the whole thing under Franz's tail. Oliver scowled—was she making *another* Christmas present?

On the other side of the room, Mama was baking. She pushed a piece of hair out of her face, whitening the strand of hair with flour. "Oliver, can you help me for a second? I've got to finish these cookies so I can pack up my baking supplies tomorrow. Can you grab me another bag of flour?"

Oliver opened the pantry door and dragged a twenty-pound flour bag over to Mama.

"I'm going to the basketball courts," Oliver reminded her before she could rope him into helping more.

"Look both ways before you cross the street, okay? And be back in an hour."

"Yeah, yeah."

"Oliver," his mom warned. "One hour."

"You *could* get me a phone," Oliver suggested, grabbing a handful of chocolate chips from the bag on the counter. "Then you wouldn't worry so much."

"I never worry," Mama said. "And absolutely no phone. I survived without a cell phone until after college."

"That's because cell phones weren't invented way back then," Oliver said, then ducked and ran to the front door when Mama aimed a piece of cookie dough at him.

"Oh, Oliver?" Mama called. "I'm going to need some help later, so don't be late."

Oliver made a face as he shrugged on his puffy blue jacket and laced up his gym sneakers, shoes his sisters described as "disgusting" and "foul." He exited the brownstone and went down the block to the park. At the end of the block, the Baptist choir was rehearsing Christmas carols, their rich voices spilling out into the neighborhood from the open church door.

Across the street from the Baptist church was a park with two basketball courts, a playground, and a grassy path lined with benches. In the summer, the older people of the neighborhood liked to sit on benches and scold the teenagers who cruised by on dirt bikes. The shaved-ice guy would stroll through, pushing his cart and ringing his bell right next to the mango lady, who sold peeled mangoes on sticks. The mango flesh was a brilliant orange color, and when Oliver bit into it, the sticky juice would drip down the mango and onto his clothes.

In the winter, no one really went to the park except dog owners, who had no other choice, and Oliver's basketball buddies, who believed that a day without a basketball game was not a day worth living.

"Hey, Oliver!" Jimmy L and some of their buddies from school were already racing up and down the courts. Oliver jogged over and Jimmy L passed him the ball. Oliver dribbled and went for a shot, only to be blocked by Angie.

Angie turned and beamed an I-can't-help-it-if-I'm-that-good smile at Oliver. She was the best basketball player in the third grade, and probably even fourth grade too. The kids proceeded to push and shove and block and dribble and fake each other out. Oliver wasn't handling the ball with his usual ease, but at least the game was taking his mind off his life. That is, until it started to get windy and his hands cramped from the cold. He knew he needed to get home before his mom showed up and embarrassed him in front of all his friends.

"You're off your game today," Jimmy L remarked to Oliver.

"I've got troubles," Oliver replied, rubbing the place on his stomach where Angie had elbowed him.

"Yeah? Hey, did you get more signatures yesterday after we left?"

Oliver nodded; then he reluctantly told the small crowd that had gathered around him about the Christmas-present dilemma.

"You need a present for Isa?" Jimmy L asked, raising his eyebrows.

"All my sisters," Oliver replied.

"Jessie too?" Dwayne asked, with a goofy smile on his face.

"All. My. Sisters."

Every boy in Oliver's grade had crushes on Isa and Jessie. It was disgusting.

"How about jewelry?" Angie suggested, jogging up to Oliver after completing a flawless lay-up. "Girls like that kind of stuff."

"*You* never wear jewelry," Oliver pointed out.

"It gets in the way of basketball," Angie replied with a shrug, spinning the ball on her index finger.

Oliver shook his head. "I have two dollars and thirty-six cents total to spend on my sisters and my parents."

His friends winced. Realizing the gravity of the situation, they started rummaging around in their pockets and backpacks for anything they could contribute to the cause. Things got pushed into Oliver's hands. One stick of peppermint gum. Two dimes and three pennies. A beat-up piece of candy. A bright green mechanical pencil with a nubby pink eraser at the end. A strand of plastic gold beads shaped like hexagons. A rock flecked with silver. Three red rubber bands in varying sizes and widths. A small bottle of hand sanitizer.

"Wow. Thanks, guys!" Oliver said happily.

"Christmas dilemma officially solved," Jimmy L announced.

Oliver agreed as he shoved everything into his jacket pockets, gave high-fives to his buddies, and headed back home. *Those are the best friends I'll ever have* was Oliver's first thought. Then, *This Beiderman thing better work.*

* * *

I'll tell Isa about Benny this afternoon, Jessie promised herself. At the moment, Isa was in the dungeon practicing her violin and Jessie was perched at the top of the basement stairs, a new experiment spread out before her. She was trying to make a fruit battery out of lemons, nails, wires, and pennies.

Isa paused from her violin playing and looked up at Jessie. "Are you going to electrocute yourself?"

"Of course not." Jessie squinted at the objects spread around her. "Maybe." She shrugged, unconcerned.

"Why don't you work on that down here?"

Jessie fiddled with her wires. "You know the probability of getting me down there is point oh one percent, right?" she replied.

"C'mon, Jess," Isa said. "We might be moving soon. I want to share this with you." Silence. "Please, Jess? Don't you love me?" she wheedled.

Jessie sighed and stood up. "Fine. But only because you identified my greatest weakness."

Jessie inched down the stairs, glancing around as if waiting for something with venomous tentacles to drop on her head and inject poison into her bloodstream. When she got to the bottom, however, her fears vanished.

"Isa, wow," she breathed. "This is . . . magical."

"I knew you would like it!" Isa gloated. Isa's eyes followed Jessie as she walked slowly around the basement, running her fingers through thick, nubby carpets hung on the wall and gently touching delicate silver stars strung above. While Jessie took it all in, Isa began to play a tender Beethoven concerto, her violin ringing through the basement. Jessie felt the music go straight into her heart. Never had Jessie heard Isa's violin sound better, and she knew it was from the homemade acoustical treatment her sister had created in the basement over the years. Everything about the space breathed life and happiness and beauty.

When Isa's piece ended, she lifted her bow off the strings and Jessie watched her twin drift back to earth.

"Sounds pretty great down here, right?" Isa said, grinning at Jessie.

"It's . . . mind-blowing," Jessie admitted.

Isa started wiping down her violin with the soft cloth she kept in her case. The violin actually belonged to Mr. Van Hooten. It was a three-quarters-size instrument that had been in his family for generations. With no one using it, he was lending it to Isa until she went up to a new size. At first she hadn't even wanted to touch it—the wood was hundreds of years old!—but when she had tried it, the sound was so pure and so lovely that she couldn't bear to let it go.

"It took me six years to get down here," Jessie said, ashamed. "I'm sorry, Isa."

Isa tilted her head. "You don't have to be sorry. I'm glad you're here now."

"You put so much work into making this place beautiful. I didn't even help you. And now it's so perfect and your violin sounds so lovely . . ."

"Hey," Isa said, "you're always around when I need you. You've always stood up for me when it mattered. Remember Jefferson Jamison?"

Jessie remembered Jefferson Jamison, all right. Last spring Isa had had a solo violin part in the school concert. Jessie had been heading backstage to wish her good luck before she performed when she overheard Jefferson Jamison talking to someone. Jefferson was one of the "cool" eighth-graders who never took off his letterman jacket and always had a crowd of girls following him around.

"These concerts are so boring," Jefferson had said to a girl with long wispy hair and tiny ears. "I wish they would cut the snooze music. Especially that violin player. What's her name? Izzy?"

Jessie had been shocked. Snooze music indeed! Dvořák's "Humoresque" was one of the most beautiful pieces ever written! How dare he insult Dvořák *and* her sister! Jessie peeked around the curtain to see Isa looking stunned and uncertain. Jessie felt the telltale signs of her temper rising as hot blood rushed through her body.

Jefferson and the girl were laughing when Jessie marched straight up to him and punched him in the arm. Hard.

Jefferson stumbled back. "What the—"

"You want to repeat that, jerk face?" Jessie had said, jabbing her index finger in the middle of the big *A* on Jefferson's letterman jacket. Jefferson was too dumbfounded to say anything to this tiny sixth-grader with big black glasses and crazy hair getting in his face.

"You were talking about my sister," Jessie had said between gritted teeth, "who just happens to be the most brilliant sixth grade violinist in the whole entire world. Maybe you smashed your head too many times on the football field, but even someone who has never heard quality music would know that Dvořák's 'Humoresque' is a work of genius. I suggest you stop strutting around in that dumb-looking jacket and get some culture!"

Jessie had spun around, her backpack full of thick science books smacking Jefferson in the ribs, and walked away. "And another thing," Jessie had said over her shoulder to a slumping Jefferson. "After my sister plays, I better see you applaud. I'm watching you."

Isa had been called to the stage at that very moment. When she stepped into the spotlight, she looked confident and radiant. Then Isa lifted her violin and played "Humoresque" like she had never played it before. It was an unforgettable moment.

Jessie shook off the memory and looked at Isa, who was now sitting on the carpet next to her. "I never asked you how you felt after playing at that concert," Jessie said.

"It was amazing. This is going to sound crazy, but I felt your strength flow through me when I was playing. See, Jessie, you make me strong. Sometimes I think you know every thought that goes through my head."

Jessie didn't respond. She wanted to believe that she was a good sister, but she couldn't shake the guilt about Benny. "Isa, I have to—"

"Do you think the brownstone loves us?" Isa interrupted, so caught up in her own thoughts she didn't hear her sister. "I do," she continued, wiping a tear from her eye.

Jessie swallowed. Obviously this was the wrong time to bring up Benny.

Isa leaned back so she was lying in the middle of the carpet. "Here, let me show you something. Lie down next to me."

Jessie dropped down next to Isa so they were head to foot.

"Listen," Isa said.

"What am I—"

"Shhh. Just listen."

Jessie watched the stars glitter above her. She heard the pipes of the brownstone clinking lightly as they carried water inside and outside their home. Next to her, Isa breathed in and out in a steady rhythm. After a few minutes, Jessie almost felt as if she could hear the brownstone's heartbeat. And she knew, just knew, that if she could save Isa's basement, then the Benny thing would be okay too.

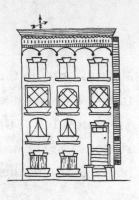

Fourteen

When Oliver returned from the basketball game, he snuck past the kitchen, where Mama was mixing away. The noise from the mixer's motor made it easy for him to race up the stairs without Mama noticing.

Back in his bedroom, Oliver pulled on the arm warmers that Hyacinth had made for him and took out the donated gifts from his friends. He was delegating the red rubber bands to Laney when his mom called to him from the kitchen. Oliver swept the gifts into his desk drawer, then grabbed his earphones and put them in, hoping that his mom would be too tired to climb the stairs in search for him.

It was not to be. Twenty seconds later, his mom opened the door and peeked inside.

"Hey, you," she said. "Want to do me a favor?"

Oliver sighed and removed the headphones. "Actually—"

"Great," said Mama. She handed him an enormous basket of cookies, all packaged in clear cellophane with jaunty little tags. Every year Mama made enough Christmas cookies to feed the entire population of Harlem, and ever since he could remember, she appointed him the distributor.

"Mama, can't someone else do it? Whenever I pass your cookies out, people want me to come in and look at photos of their grandkids and talk to me forever."

"That's why I included sustenance!" Mama reached into the baskct and pulled out a bag labeled "OLI-VER." The bag contained all six kinds of cookies he liked best. Mama sure fought dirty when she wanted to.

"All right. Go on now," Mama said. On her way out of his bedroom, she grabbed a stack of books off one of his shelves and put them into the empty moving box she had left in his room earlier that day. Then she disappeared out the door, and Oliver could hear her weaving around the growing number of boxes stacked against the hallway wall. Oliver put the books back on his bookshelf, shoved a few petition papers into his back pocket, then stumbled down the stairs with the enormous basket.

"Have a fun time, honey!" Mama called from the kitchen. Oliver grunted. He braced himself against the cold, then let himself outside.

First stop: Mr. Smiley, the super at the building two doors down and the father of Angie, his basketball buddy. Oliver staggered to the sidewalk and made his way over.

"Oliver!"

Oliver looked up to see Angie waving at him from the stoop of her building. She bounded down the steps like a gazelle and landed at his feet. He put his basket down and greeted her with their special basketball handshake, a complicated series of backhand slaps and finger pointing, ending with tilting their heads over their shoulders and saying "Oh yeah!"

After that particular ritual was over, Oliver leaned down and pulled out the bag of cookies his mom had made for their family. "For you," Oliver said.

Angie grabbed them and wasted no time opening the

bag and removing a sugar cookie decorated like a Christmas tree. She took a bite and closed her eyes. "I love your mom's cookies," she said when she was done chewing. "Hey, can I come with you to drop the cookies off? We can get more signatures for your petition."

Oliver nodded. "Sounds good. Hey, did I tell you that the Beiderman started showing the apartment to new people already?"

Angie's eyes widened. "Don't you have tenant rights or something? My dad is always talking about tenant and landlord rights."

"Mama says our lease is only good until the end of the year. He's allowed to rent to someone else if he wants."

"There must be a way to stop him," Angie said, tapping her fingers against her chin. "Have you done an Internet search on the Beiderman yet?"

Oliver nodded. "We tried, but our Internet got shut off."

"My dad will let us use his computer." Without waiting for Oliver to respond, Angie grabbed one of the two handles of the cookie basket and together they lugged it to Angie's apartment.

They opened the door to find her father, Mr. Smiley, sitting in his armchair flipping through a dog-eared dictionary.

"Are those Mrs. Vanderbeeker's holiday cookies?" Mr. Smiley asked, rising from his seat.

Angie gave her dad the squinty eye before pulling the bag of cookies from her pocket and handing it over. "Don't eat them all," she warned. "Oliver and I are going to use the computer." She tossed her jacket onto an empty chair and sat down at the living room table, where an ancient monitor sat attached to a whirring hard drive.

Oliver flopped into the seat next to her. "Does that thing even work? It looks a million years old."

"It got a lot better after Jessie fiddled with it," Angie said, pulling up the Internet search engine, which opened at once.

Oliver didn't have time to be amazed at Jessie's apparent genius around computers, because Angie had already typed *Beiderman* into the search function. They didn't know his first name, so they added *Harlem*, and then *City College*. Angie scrolled and scanned, then punched more keys. Oliver watched the screen until his eyes glazed over. This was taking *forever*.

"Hey," Oliver interrupted after what seemed like hours. "My mom will kill me if I don't deliver these cookies. You still in?"

Angie took one last look at the search results, then reluctantly closed down the search engine. "I'll do more tonight," she promised before grabbing her coat and entering the living room. "Dad, I'm going to help Oliver with the cookie deliveries!"

Mr. Smiley, startled to see the kids, hastily stuffed an empty cellophane cookie bag behind the couch cushion before flashing them a guilty smile. A scattering of crumbs clung to his beard.

Angie pointed an accusing finger at him. "Da-ad! You ate *all* of them?"

When Mr. Smiley could only offer a sheepish shrug, Angie rolled her eyes and stomped out the door.

Oliver followed her. He looked at his cookie bag, and then at Angie. In an act of supreme sacrifice, he tapped her on the shoulder. When she turned around, he held the bag out to her. "You can have some of mine. I don't mind," he lied.

"Really? Thanks!" Angie took a cookie (it happened to be the one Oliver would have chosen to eat next himself) and nibbled off an end. Oliver sighed. Sometimes it was just so hard to be nice.

Two hours later, the cookies were delivered, and Oliver had been grateful for Angie's company. It was exhausting remembering his manners when talking to all those people, but Angie smiled and chatted as if she didn't mind seeing the same baby over and over in two dozen pictures.

The cookie basket was empty save one bag, and they had gathered twenty more signatures on the petition. Oliver gave Angie *another* cookie from his personal supply, leaving him with only two. Oliver could not wait to go back home, sit alone in his bedroom, read *Prince Caspian,* and eat those last two cookies in peace.

"If you want to leave those petition sheets for me, I'll get more people to sign," Angie offered.

Oliver handed over the petitions, then walked back to the brownstone. He had one last bag to deliver, this time to someone in his own building. The label said "Mr. Beiderman" in his mom's swirly handwriting. Oliver trudged up to the third floor. When he got there, he saw a bag of trash hanging on the handle of the Beiderman's apartment. He knew his father came up to the third floor a few times a week to collect the Beiderman's garbage and bring it down to the building trash bins. Oliver unhooked the bag from the doorknob and left the bag of cookies in front of the door.

Halfway down the stairs, Oliver turned around, climbed back up to the third floor, and placed his own bag of cookies down next to the one he had just left there.

"Peace offering," Oliver said out loud.

There was no response from the other side of the door—Oliver didn't expect there would be—so he headed back downstairs. Something inside the garbage bag made a funny clinking sound, so naturally Oliver peeked in to see what it was.

Scattered among the remains of frozen dinners were shards of a broken record.

❋ ❋ ❋

"Two days left for Operation Beiderman," Isa said from her spot by the easel in the twins' room. "We need to diversify our strategy."

"We got a bunch of signatures for the petitions," Jessie said as she fiddled with an old computer hard drive she had found on the curb.

"It's not enough," Isa said. She drew a diagram on the whiteboard and wrote "Beiderman Strategy" in big letters in the middle, then drew two arrows pointing outward. One arrow pointed to "Petition." At the end of the second arrow, she wrote "Acts of Kindness."

Oliver groaned when he saw Isa's last addition. "Can't we sabotage the people who want to rent our apartment? That's a lot more fun."

"I know the other nice things we did for him did not go as planned," Isa said, "but the petition can only do so much. It tells the Beiderman that people like us in the neighborhood, but it doesn't tell him *why*. We have to *persuade* him to like us. We need to appeal to his heart."

"Technically, it's the brain that processes emotion, not the heart," Jessie pointed out.

"You know what I mean," Isa replied.

"I left the little Christmas tree outside his door," Laney said while sucking on a strand of her hair.

"Don't suck on your hair," Isa said, followed by, "That was very sweet of you."

"*And* me and Oliver left him a record. A *jazz* record," Laney added.

Isa raised her eyebrows. "A jazz record? Cool."

"Miss Josie said he liked jazz," Laney said breezily.

"I can't believe I never thought to ask Miss Josie about him," Jessie said. "Of course. They've lived here even longer than he has."

Oliver was not about to share what he'd discovered inside the Beiderman's trash and break Laney's heart. "Angie tried to search for him on the Internet," he reported instead, "but she didn't come up with anything yet."

"What is wrong with me?" Jessie said to no one. "I should have asked Angie if I could use their computer."

"I also gave him some of my cookies," Oliver said.

The room stilled.

"You . . . what?" Isa whispered.

"Cookies. Some of the ones Mama made for me."

Jessie spoke slowly. "You gave the Beiderman cookies. From your own personal stash. Willingly. Not under duress."

"Wow," Hyacinth said in wonder. Franz's tail thumped on the floor.

"I'm so proud," Isa announced. "Such sacrifice."

Oliver's face turned red. "Can we just keep going with the meeting?"

Hyacinth spoke up. "Mr. Jones said the Beiderman used to teach art at the castle college. No, not art." She tilted her head, thinking. "Art *history*."

"We should contact the art history department at City College," Isa said. "Maybe someone knows him there."

"Art history sounds so boring," Oliver remarked.

"I think it sounds romantic," Isa said. "I would love to know more about what life was like when Vincent van Gogh and Pablo Picasso lived."

"That's because you have an artist's soul," Jessie said. "The right hemisphere of your brain is very highly developed."

"Yeah. Art history is boring to those of us with normal brains," Oliver chimed in.

"I like art," Laney interrupted. "I want to learn about it."

"Thank you," Isa said primly.

"I think we should go to the art history department," Isa repeated. "Maybe tomorrow when we go out with the petitions again."

Laney's face lit up. "We get to go to the castle?" The last time the Vanderbeekers went to the castle was for a spring fair their school was hosting with the college. Laney was only two at the time, and to her disgust she didn't remember anything about it.

"Sounds good to me," said Jessie.

"Great. Now, what I was *going* to say before we got sidetracked"—Isa gave Oliver a pointed look—"is that we need to give the Beiderman a more personal look into who we are."

"How?" Oliver asked suspiciously. "I'm not giving up any more cookies, if that's what you're thinking."

"We need to wow him with how great we are," said Isa. "So he wouldn't be able to imagine anyone as awesome as us living here."

"I'm good at hugging people," Laney announced.

"I can't see hugging the Beiderman going well right now," said Jessie.

"Maybe you can draw him a picture of the brownstone," Isa suggested. "Who doesn't love a picture drawn by a four-year-old?"

Laney's brow creased. "I'm four and three-quarters," she corrected Isa.

"I can make him something science-y," offered Jessie.

"I'll write him a poem," Oliver said. His sisters stared at him. "What?" Oliver said defensively. "Poetry is cool, okay?"

"I wonder if I should make him a CD of my violin playing," said Isa. "I'm so much better than I was six years ago."

Hyacinth kept her head down, pretending to inspect Franz for fleas.

"Don't forget we need to continue collecting even more signatures," Isa reminded them. "It's a lot, but we can do it!"

Oliver started humming the *Star Wars* theme song.

"No obstacle is too big," Isa continued as Oliver increased his humming volume.

"No man too mean," Jessie added.

"We are the Vanderbeekers!" piped up Hyacinth as Oliver reached a crescendo in his song.

"Let's save our home!" declared Isa.

MONDAY, DECEMBER 23

Fifteen

We're going for a walk," Jessie announced to her mom.

"Take Laney with you," Mama called out from the kitchen. "Please," she added with a note of desperation.

On every available inch of counter space, and on every available inch of the kitchen floor, lay Mama's baking supplies, ready for packing. Laney was having a wonderful time examining each item and organizing the supplies for her own personal "store." She had found a stack of sticky notes and priced items anywhere from one cent to three hundred thousand dollars.

Papa emerged from the bathroom, where he was sanding down the walls in preparation for a new coat of paint.

"I think you officially have every baking utensil ever invented," Papa said, looking at the clutter of the kitchen. He picked up a metal pincher thing with needle-like tips. "What *is* this?"

"It's a fondant crimper. Don't let Laney have it," Mama replied as she watched him hand it to Laney.

"Ooh, fun," Laney said, squeezing it together.

"Please, Isa. Save my life here," Mama pleaded.

"Laney, let's go for a walk," Isa suggested, plucking the fondant crimper out of Laney's hands and handing it back to Mama.

"We could check out City College," Isa said in a singsong voice as she took Laney's coat off the coat hook and held it out to her.

"Yay, the castle!" Laney said, jumping to her feet. She looked at Mama. "We're going to find out if—"

"—princesses live there," Isa cut in.

"Okay," Mama said as she packed up the fondant crimper. She did not say "Be careful!" or "Be back in an hour or else!" so the kids knew she was very distracted.

A northeastern wind had joined the cold front, and it felt twenty degrees colder than the day before. Whenever a gust passed, the kids turned so their backs served as shields against the wind. No one spoke—hats were pulled low and scarves were pulled high.

The smell of Castleman's Bakery tempted the Vanderbeekers when they passed by, and each Vanderbeeker felt noble as they resisted the desire to take shelter in the cozy store. They crossed the street and stood before the college entrance. Imposing wrought-iron gates reached skyward, and beyond the gates was the college campus. Up close, the buildings were more intimidating than they were from the brownstone roof. Instead of being like a princess's home, the buildings looked like they belonged on a craggy cliff above a raging sea during a lightning storm.

The Vanderbeekers looked at each other. Finally, Isa shrugged and stepped inside the gates. Her siblings followed her down a cobblestone path toward the center of campus. When they emerged in the enormous courtyard, they found the college almost deserted.

"Wow," said Oliver. "Where are the people?"

"I think this college is closed," Hyacinth said.

"I'm sure people are still working," Isa said in her falsely cheery voice. "There must be a map somewhere . . ."

"I see it! I see a map!" Laney said. She dragged Isa by the hand to an information post.

"Look, they have a whole department just for chemistry," Jessie said reverently, looking over Laney's shoulder as she examined the map. "That's awesome."

"And a music department too," Isa said.

"Let me see," said Oliver, crowding in.

"Ah! Here it is! The art history department. It's in Goethals Hall." Isa looked away from the map and surveyed the campus. "That one."

To Laney's disappointment, Goethals Hall wasn't the huge castle building visible from the Vanderbeekers' brownstone roof. Instead, it was like a miniature version of the more impressive castle. The kids made their way to the building, and it took the strength of both Oliver and Jessie to push the heavy wooden doors open wide enough for the rest of the kids to squeeze inside. The black iron hinges groaned. The temperature inside was only slightly warmer than outside, and the interior seemed to be made entirely of cold marble: marble floors, marble walls, and, before them, a long marble staircase.

The kids wandered around, lost for ten minutes before they ran into a student in plaid flannel pajama bottoms and boots that looked like house slippers.

"Do you know where the art history department is?" Jessie asked him.

The guy pointed. "Two floors up, make a right. The office is at the end of the hall."

The kids followed his directions, and sure enough, a door at the end of the second-floor hallway had a piece of paper with "ART HISTORY" written on it in fat marker. Isa peeked in. A woman with graying hair pulled into a severe bun sat behind a wooden desk that took up nearly the whole room. The top of the desk was completely empty except for a shallow box filled with papers in one corner and a desktop computer in the other.

"Just put it in the box," she said in a monotone voice, not looking up from her computer. *Tap tap tap.*

Isa stepped into the room. "I'm sorry to be a bother, but I just have one quick question."

"You're about to be late with your paper. Either turn it in now or fail the class," she replied. *Tap tap tap.*

"But I'm not in a class," Isa replied. "I have a question about someone who might have worked here."

Finally, the woman looked at the Vanderbeekers. "Kids are not supposed to be here," she said, her pencil-thin eyebrows raising up to her hairline.

"We have a question," Isa repeated, slowly. "We were wondering if you know of a Mr. Beiderman. He used to work in this department."

"Never heard of him," the woman replied, going back to her computer. "Where are your parents?" *Tap tap tap.*

"We're doing research on our neighbor," Jessie chimed in, stepping inside the office, followed by Oliver, Hyacinth, and Laney. "He might have worked here six years ago."

"I told you I never heard of him, and I've worked here for five years." *Tap tap tap.*

"Is there anyone who would have been here six or seven years ago who might know?" Isa pressed.

"Nope. Faculty left last week. Final papers are due right now, and in ten seconds I'm packing these essays up and mailing them off to Professor Suarez's home. The college will be closed until January fifteenth. You can come back then." *Tap tap tap.*

"January fifteenth?" Jessie exclaimed. "You can't look it up on your computer right now?"

The lady stopped tapping and powered down her computer. "Sorry."

She did not sound one bit sorry. The Vanderbeekers watched as she slid the papers from her desk into a manila envelope.

From the hallway, the Vanderbeekers heard someone yell, "Wait! I have it!"

The kids peeked out the door and saw a disheveled girl racing toward them, waving a paper. When the girl reached them, she grabbed hold of the doorway to stop her momentum. The Vanderbeekers parted to let her inside. "I have my paper!" she gasped.

"Too late," the gray-haired lady replied. She pointed at the clock. It was 10:01 a.m.

The girl clutched her heart. "Please! I have to pass this class or I'll lose my scholarship!"

"Everyone out of my office," the ruiner of hopes replied. "My winter break started one minute ago." The lady grabbed her jacket and purse from the coat rack, then pushed everyone out of the office and into the hallway. She followed them and closed the door behind her. After she locked it, she took a last look at the dejected group of people around her.

To Isa and Jessie she said, "Come back in January, after the fifteenth. Maybe someone can help you then."

To the girl with the paper—who was now wringing her hands and crying—the gray-haired woman snapped, "Next time, don't be late." Then she yanked the essay out of the student's hand and clicked down the hallway, disappearing around a corner.

"Oh, thank goodness," the frazzled student said, slumping down against the wall.

The Vanderbeekers shook their heads in wonder. College was looking more and more like a place where dreams came to die.

"There are no princesses here," Laney said, tears leaking out of her eyes as she followed her siblings out of the building.

"Oh, Laney, I'm sorry. This was my terrible idea," Isa said, picking Laney up and drying her little sister's eyes. "Do you want to go to Castleman's? I'll buy you a cookie."

Laney shook her head, her hair tumbling into her face. "I want to go home."

The Vanderbeekers began to trudge back to 141st Street, all illusions about the magic of the castle college lost forever. They yearned for the warmth of their home, the pets awaiting their arrival, the comfort of Mama's nourishing meals, and the love of their friends and neighbors.

❖ ❖ ❖

It was a quiet walk back to 141st Street. When they arrived at their block, Jessie paused to get a signature for the petition from their neighbor Charlotte and her son Joseph. While five-year-old Joseph carefully inscribed his name on a line, a middle-aged man in a worn overcoat and swathed in a bright red scarf approached them.

"Want to sign our petition?" asked Laney, approaching him and unearthing another crumpled petition from her coat pocket.

The man's eyes crinkled kindly as he looked at the five kids standing before him. He took the paper and unfolded it.

"Hello," the man said in a deep, gravelly voice. "Tell me about your petition."

The kids introduced themselves. "We're trying to convince our landlord to renew our lease," Isa explained.

"Surely," he said, signing "Mr. Austin Rochester" on an open line without bothering to read the top. "I applaud your civic-mindedness," said Mr. Rochester. A blast of arctic wind came through, and Mr. Rochester and the kids turned their backs to it. When the wind eased, he continued. "I love seeing people get involved in their community. I always try to encourage that in my work."

"Where do you work?" asked Hyacinth.

"I'm a musician," said Mr. Rochester. "I play the cello, and I conduct an orchestra for teens called Rhythm NYC."

"I've heard of that!" said Isa, her eyes brightening. "I'm a musician too. I play the violin!"

"If you're in high school, you can audition," encouraged Mr. Rochester.

"I'm only twelve. But in two years I'm totally going to audition. It sounds amazing."

Mr. Rochester reached into his coat pocket and pulled out a business card. "Keep this, and be sure to audition the summer before your freshman year. All the information is on our website."

Isa cradled the business card as if it were a priceless gift.

"Do you live around here?" asked Oliver.

"No, but I'm looking at an apartment in this area. It's in a brownstone." He showed Oliver the address. "Am I going in the right direction?"

Isa, Jessie, Hyacinth, and Laney watched Oliver read the address, then glance up at them with panicked eyes.

"Uh, actually, you need to go three avenue blocks

that way," Oliver lied, pointing in the opposite direction.

"Thank you very much! I have the worst sense of direction. My wife is always leading me everywhere. She's traveling in Egypt right now, doing research on mummies. Cool, right?"

"Cool," echoed the children.

"Well, I better get going. I have a rehearsal right after I see the apartment, and I'm already running late," he said, looking at his watch. "It was very nice meeting you all." Mr. Rochester shook all the kids' hands, accepted a hug from Laney, then strode away from them and the brownstone.

"Lightning might strike me down right here," said Oliver.

"He was so nice," Isa said with tears in her eyes. "And we just . . . just . . . lied to him!"

"It was for a good reason," Jessie said weakly.

"I want him to be our neighbor," declared Laney. "His wife knows about mummies!"

"He would have been perfect for the brownstone," Isa said mournfully. "He would have understood the spirit of it."

A particularly brutal wind swept through and the Vanderbeekers didn't bother turning their backs to avoid the sting on their cheeks. It felt like a well-deserved punishment.

Sixteen

Later that afternoon, the siblings worked on their Acts of Kindness projects. Laney sat at the living room table making her brownstone drawing, with Hyacinth, Jessie, and Oliver next to her. Franz lay under the table, keeping an eye out for Paganini, who had taken to drinking from his water bowl. Downstairs in the basement, Isa was recording her violin CD. After ten minutes of silent work, Hyacinth looked over at Laney's progress.

"Is that supposed to be our home?" Hyacinth asked.

"Yup," said Laney, the tip of her tongue sticking out the side of her mouth.

Jessie peeked over from where she was working on her fruit battery experiment. "Our brownstone is not rainbow-colored."

"Nope," said Laney, adding a violet stripe in the middle of the building.

"The Beiderman won't even know what that is!" scoffed Oliver.

"Sure he will! It's the brownstone!"

"Don't you think it should be more . . . realistic?" Jessie suggested. "Here, let me help—"

"I'm doing it *my* way," Laney said, pushing Jessie's hand away.

Laney pursed her lips in a stubborn line as she continued her drawing. Soon the entire page filled with color. Along the bottom she had drawn her family (including the animals), Miss Josie and Mr. Jeet, and what she thought the Beiderman looked like.

Hyacinth didn't want to reveal her *real* plan for the Beiderman—it was top secret—so instead she made a Christmas wreath with cardboard and tissue paper. As she glued small puffs of rolled-up tissue paper onto a cardboard circle, a thought came to her. "Why do you think the Beiderman never leaves his apartment?"

Jessie shrugged. "He's a crabby old man who hates everyone."

"That doesn't make sense. We know other crabby people who leave their apartments."

"Mr. Nelson is super-*duper* crabby," Laney reported, thinking about the guy who manned the booth at their local subway station. "It's 'cause he has arithmetic."

There was a brief pause. "*Arthritis,*" Jessie corrected her.

"Does the Beezerman have that too?"

"There has to be a bigger reason for not ever leaving your apartment," Oliver said. "Maybe he's on house arrest," he suggested, his eyes brightening. "Or . . . maybe he's in the Witness Protection Program!"

"Uncle Arthur needs to stop sending you mysteries," Jessie said.

Oliver ignored her and waved a piece of paper in the air. Hyacinth had given him stationery with drawings of pandas all over it for his poem, which Oliver thought was weird but his sisters insisted was cute. "Hey, how does this haiku sound?"

I haven't bounced my
basketball in forty days
Do you feel the peace?
The Great Commander
Oliver S. Vanderbeeker

"It's a little ... brief," Jessie said as she sifted through a box of odds and ends she had picked up over the years. Bolts, bent nails, tubing, rusting pennies, and orphaned keys were all jumbled together.

Oliver rolled his eyes. "Hello? It's a haiku. Five syllables, seven syllables, five syllables." He signed it with a flourish.

Meanwhile, Jessie gathered four lemons and six pieces of wire that were connected on each side to small alligator clips. She clipped the wires to the lemons by attaching one end to a nail on one lemon and the other end to a penny on the next lemon. Pretty soon all four lemons were connected, and the wires on the ends dangled free.

Jessie looked at her siblings. "Are you ready?" she asked. They nodded eagerly.

Jessie touched the remaining wires to two small prongs coming down from an LED light, and the light blinked on.

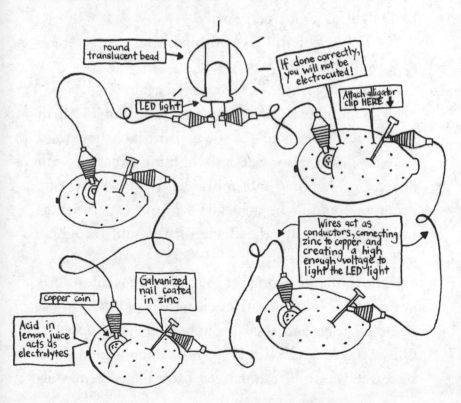

"Wow wow wow!" Laney yelled, reaching out to touch it. Jessie swatted her hand away.

"That's so cool," Hyacinth said. "The Beiderman will be amazed."

"Is that all it does?" Oliver asked, unimpressed.

"I'm going to stick this cool bead on it." Jessie nudged a translucent emerald-green bead onto the LED light so it glowed prettily.

"Ooh, I *love* that," Hyacinth said.

"I want one too," Laney said.

"Is that all it does?" Oliver asked again.

Jessie shrugged. The effect was less dramatic than she would have liked—if she'd had time, she would have created a more elaborate lighting situation with dozens of lemons and more lights—but scientific progress couldn't be achieved without experimentation, and hopefully the Beiderman would recognize and appreciate the effort.

Jessie took one prong off the nail of one lemon so as not to waste valuable citric acids, then laid her project out on a tray, and they brought their gifts upstairs. Oliver stayed back with Hyacinth on the second floor, since she was still traumatized from the placemat disaster. Laney's drawing and Oliver's poem were shoved under the door, Hyacinth's wreath was taped up under the peephole, and Jessie settled her tray on the floor. Then she slipped another note under the door. It read, "Check outside and be surprised!"

As Hyacinth watched her sisters set everything up, she only hoped she could be brave enough to go to the Beiderman's door too, when the time was right.

❖ ❖ ❖

The doorbell rang a few minutes after the kids returned. Franz sprinted toward the door, not realizing that the rug by the door had been packed up. He skidded against the wood floor and slammed into the wall. Jessie nudged him aside.

"Hey, Angie," Jessie said, opening the door and letting her in. Franz recovered after a brisk shake and circled Angie, his tail registering 200 wpm.

"Is Oliver here?" Angie asked, unwrapping her scarf and scratching Franz behind the ears.

"Yup." Jessie yelled behind her. "Oliver, the girl who kicks your butt at basketball is here!"

Oliver came out of the kitchen with a thick peanut butter and jelly sandwich in his hand. "Hey. What's up?" he said around a mouthful of sticky sandwich.

Angie looked at him with solemn eyes. "I found out something about the Beiderman."

Oliver stopped chewing. Jessie ran to the basement stairs and yelled for Isa, who was still recording her CD. Soon all the Vanderbeeker kids surrounded Angie.

Oliver swallowed. "What is it? What did you find out?"

Angie handed Oliver a sheet of paper. It was a computer printout with a few brief lines of text.

Oliver read it out loud. "'Abigail Beiderman, forty-two, and daughter Luciana, sixteen, Harlem residents, died on March eighth, 2007. They are survived by husband and father, Arthur Beiderman. Arrangements under the direction of Bernard's Funeral Home.'" He looked at Angie. "Do you think this Arthur Beiderman is *our* Beiderman?"

"I'm almost positive this is your Beiderman. My dad recognized the first name."

"He had a kid? And a wife?" Isa asked.

"It can't be him," Jessie said. "He hates kids. He hates people."

"What if he" — Oliver paused dramatically — "killed them?"

Hyacinth gasped. Franz growled. Laney stuck her pinkies in her ears.

"If he killed them," Jessie pointed out, "he would be in jail."

"Only if they found him," Angie chimed in. "Maybe that's why he never comes out of his apartment! He's hiding!"

"No, no, no," Isa said. "He wouldn't be hiding where he lived. He would be on some remote island off the coast of Mexico, or Madagascar, or something."

"True," Oliver admitted, looking back down at the obituary. His eyes kept focusing on the word *died*. It seemed so final.

"I wonder how they died," Jessie said. "Strange that his wife *and* daughter died but he didn't."

"Isn't that so sad?" Isa asked. "Can you imagine if we all died and only Papa was left? What would Papa do?"

"Papa would cry," Laney said. "He would cry, and cry, and cry."

The kids fell silent, imagining what it would be like to have your family die and be the only one left living.

✳ ✳ ✳

Isa had a black-hole feeling in her stomach. It was only three o'clock and nothing was going right. First the failure to get in touch with the art history department at City College. Then the whole lying-to-a-super-nice-person-for-selfish-reasons situation with Mr. Rochester. Finally, most of all, discovering that the Beiderman's family was dead.

Her mind was a tornado of thoughts and questions and anxiety while she recorded herself playing the violin section of Paganini's "Cantabile for Violin and Guitar" for the CD she was making for the Beiderman. *It's hard to play a cantabile when your mind is a tornado,* Isa thought as she started over again.

Jessie joined her in the basement not too much later. As Isa recorded her fourth take, she watched Jessie prop two pillows against the wall and sprawl against them with her *National Geographic* magazine. A few minutes later she watched Jessie slowly close her eyes, lulled to sleep by the violin playing and the warm air wrapping around her from the radiator.

Isa switched off the recorder. There was no magic in the cantabile right now. She needed to get outside, breathe fresh air, and clear her mind. She glanced at Jessie, wondering if she should wake her, but her sister looked so peaceful curled up on the carpet. Isa laid a blanket over her before heading upstairs.

Isa made her way to Castleman's to buy bread for the next day's dinner, fighting the intensifying wind the whole way. She was anxious about seeing Benny again after their super-weird conversation a couple of days ago. Benny was one of her best friends. She had spent hundreds of hours in the bakery with him, playing board games and working out puzzles. More recently, Benny was the boy who helped her find her locker and walked her to classes on the first day of middle school. How could he care so little about their move?

By the time she arrived at the bakery, Isa was surprised to feel her heart pounding. She entered to find

Mrs. Castleman—not Benny—behind the register, helping another family with an order. Isa hung back and studied the glass case even though she knew everything in it with her eyes closed. When the other customers left, Mrs. Castleman spotted Isa and gestured her over.

"I have something for you," Mrs. Castleman said, reaching under the counter and pulling out an envelope. "Read it later."

"What is it?" asked Isa, taking the envelope. It was so light, Isa wasn't sure anything was inside.

Mrs. Castleman just shook her head and disappeared through the doors into the back of the bakery. Isa froze when she heard Mrs. Castleman calling Benny to come out and handle the front.

Isa busied herself by putting the envelope in her bag, her hands trembling. When the door swung open, Isa looked up. Benny saw her, stilled, then stiffened.

"Hi," Isa said.

"Hi," Benny replied.

"I'm here to buy bread."

"Fine."

"I'll take three loaves of French bread."

"Fine."

Benny took three loaves from the basket and bagged them.

"That's four fifty."

Isa took out her wallet and gave him exact change.

"Thanks," Isa said.

Benny didn't respond, turning his back to her as he adjusted the display of breads hanging in wire baskets against the wall.

Isa took the bag and started to leave. But she was feeling reckless, an unusual emotion for her. She turned back around and stomped to the cash register.

"What exactly is your problem, Benny?" Isa demanded, hands on her hips.

Benny spun around. "What do you mean, *my problem*? How can you even ask that? *You're* the one with the problem!"

"*I* have a problem? *You're* the one acting so weird. A terrible thing is happening to me, and you don't even care."

Benny's eyes narrowed. "Nice to know I'm such a terrible thing. Thanks a lot, Isa."

"What does this have to do with *you*? I thought you would help me, not blow me off."

"*Me* blow *you* off? You're the one who—" Benny stopped and took a deep breath. "Look, Isa, let's just pretend this whole thing never happened. Okay?"

"What *thing*? You're making no sense!"

"Are you telling me you forgot about the eighth grade dance already?"

"What does the eighth grade dance have to do with me? I helped Allegra choose a dress for the dance, if that's what you're talking about. She's going with Carlson."

"I know she's going with Carlson," Benny said through gritted teeth. "I'm talking about *you*."

"*I'm* not going to the dance, Benny! No one asked me!" Isa said, her voice rising to a shout.

"*I asked you!*" Benny shouted back.

Then, silence.

"I—what—with—you?" Isa stuttered. "You never asked!"

"I did! I asked Jessie if she thought you would go with me, and she said you would definitely NOT. She was positive."

Isa's heart skipped a beat; then she whispered, "She never told me, Benny."

"Right," Benny said bitterly. "You two talk about everything. Don't act like you didn't know. Anyway, I've already asked someone else." Benny began to tidy up the area around the register, dismissing her.

Isa felt like crying. How could he think she was lying to him? Did he really want to take her to his dance? Who was he taking now?

And then there was Jessie. Her best friend, her twin sister, the person who knew her better than anyone. Or so she thought.

Isa left the bakery and blindly walked toward home, not feeling the harsh wind whipping around her. She needed to get answers.

She needed to talk to Jessie.

Seventeen

Mama was exasperated. Mr. Beiderman's real estate agent had the nerve to call about someone seeing the place tomorrow. Tomorrow! Christmas Eve! Mama said absolutely, definitely no apartment showings on Christmas Eve or Christmas Day. When the agent continued to wheedle her, Mama hung up on her. The nerve!

"I have too much to do," Mama said, talking to herself as she stood in the middle of a living room full of boxes. Oliver was sitting inside one box, reading, and Laney was sitting in another, pretending she was a puppy.

"I can help you," Hyacinth offered from her spot on the rug. Her brow was furrowed as she manipulated knitting needles, and Franz's eyes were glued to the unwinding yarn ball.

Mama glanced at the grimy basset hound. "You know, you *can* help. Franz needs a bath."

It had been three weeks since Franz's last bath. The longer Franz went without a bath, the wilder and more erratic his behavior became. He was much more contained when he had clean ears and smelled like honeysuckle.

With the swiftness of hunted gazelles, Oliver and Laney jumped out of their boxes and raced up the stairs. Their disappearances were phenomenons that happened every time Hyacinth gave Franz a bath.

Hyacinth eyed her dog. "Don't worry, Franz. This will be quick." Franz hunkered down by the back door and tried to make himself invisible.

Hyacinth lured him with her secret weapon—a dog biscuit—and Franz's stomach betrayed him as he crept toward the heavenly-smelling treat. Hyacinth grabbed his collar at the same time Franz grabbed the biscuit, and she used all her strength to drag him toward the bathroom and into the tub. Fifteen minutes later, Franz was hoarse from his persistent howling and they were both soaked. Hyacinth wrapped Franz in a fluffy towel, then braced herself and knocked on the bathroom door three times.

"Are you ready?" Hyacinth yelled.

"Not yet . . . Wait . . . Okay, I think everything is secure!" her mother yelled back.

Hyacinth opened the door a crack and peeked out. Her mom had put up an old baby gate to block the stairs leading up to the bedrooms, and Paganini had been removed to safety upstairs. Mama was standing on the other side of the baby gate, ready for Franz's appearance.

"WOOF WOOF WOOF WOOF!" Franz broadcast as he nudged his way out of the bathroom and bounded through the living room and kitchen. He bounced off sofas, knocked over chairs, and skidded into moving boxes. These post-bath rampages lasted only about ten minutes, and the Vanderbeekers knew to steer clear until Franz exhausted himself.

Unfortunately, when Hyacinth let Franz loose, she did not count on someone coming home at that exact moment. The front door opened, and in walked Isa.

"Watch out!" Hyacinth yelled at Isa.

"Franz!" Mama yelled at the crazed dog.

But it was too late. Mama shielded her eyes.

"WOOF!" barked Franz, running straight toward Isa and not stopping until he rammed right into her and knocked her down, leaving a basset hound–sized wet spot on her jacket.

"What the . . ." Isa felt something inside her snap. She pushed Franz off and struggled to her feet. Franz, who now realized that knocking Isa over was one of his poorer decisions of the year, retreated slowly to Hyacinth, who stood in the bathroom doorway, still dripping.

The commotion in the living room was so dramatic that the Vanderbeeker kids peeked down and watched as Isa marched to the head of the basement stairs, where Jessie had just appeared after waking up from her nap.

"YOU." Isa pointed a finger at Jessie. "We need to talk RIGHT NOW." Isa strode out the back entrance into the yard, the door slamming behind her.

✿ ✿ ✿

Jessie was petrified. Isa had never, ever raised her voice to her like that. She felt the eyes of her family follow her as she walked through the kitchen and into the backyard. Isa stood stiffly under the old maple, her back to Jessie. Wind gusted around them, and Jessie rubbed her arms, shivering.

"I was just at Castleman's," Isa said.

Jessie gulped.

"Guess who I saw there."

"Uh . . . Mrs. Castleman?" Jessie suggested hopefully.

"BENNY!" Isa shouted, turning to face Jessie, the wind whipping through her hair. "He hates me. All because of you."

"I can explain, Isa—"

"Do you have the right to make decisions for me? You *knew* I wanted to go to the dance. Now Benny thinks I hate him. Why would you do this to me?"

"Isa, I thought you wouldn't want to go! Remember how I used to make fun of those dances—"

"*I am not you!*" Isa yelled. "We are not the same person! And because of you, Benny asked someone else to the dance!" Tears ran down Isa's face. Jessie was a statue, unable to move or say a word.

Isa's voice lowered. "I want you to leave me alone. Don't speak to me. Don't speak for me, don't make decisions for me. Don't talk to other people about me. *Got it?*"

Isa flew back into the apartment and the door banged closed. Her family, who had watched the entire exchange through the windows, jumped guiltily away. Their eyes followed Isa as she stormed upstairs. When they heard her bedroom door slam, they returned to the windows to look for Jessie. Her back was to them, but they could see her shoulders hunched. Jessie stood out there for five minutes in the cold, with no jacket, before Mama joined her.

"Hey," Mama said, draping a coat over her. Jessie was shaking. "Want to talk? Can I help?"

Jessie shook her head. Mama put her arms around Jessie's waist, pulling her close, murmuring comforting words. Together they stood until Jessie began to shake so uncontrollably that Mama took her arm and guided her inside.

※ ※ ※

Later that evening, Jessie went to bed on the couch. Isa had made it clear she did not want to see Jessie that night, or possibly ever again. It was the first time in their lives that the twins hadn't slept in the same room. Sensing that she needed companionship, George Washington curled at Jessie's side and did not once attack her feet. Paganini lay on the floor at the foot of the couch, nose twitching and ears pricked forward, as if on alert for danger.

Tears leaked from Jessie's eyes and soaked into her pillow as she stared at the ceiling, counting the number of times she heard ambulance sirens blare down the avenue en route to the hospital. She counted eight before she settled into a troubled sleep. A few hours later, she awoke to see her father dozing on the floor next to Paganini.

"Papa," Jessie whispered, her voice rough with sleep and tears.

"Moral support," he said. "In case you need me."

Jessie closed her eyes again as more tears rolled down her cheeks.

Upstairs, Isa had yet to fall asleep. Her mind buzzed with thoughts of her sister and Benny and eighth grade dances and long pale-pink dresses and corsages. The thoughts merged into the Beiderman and their brownstone and her basement, and Isa felt so lonely and lost that she didn't know how their mission to win him over could possibly succeed.

After another hour of tossing, Isa remembered the envelope Mrs. Castleman had given her. She got out of bed and dug through her bag to find it. As she opened the envelope, a yellowed newspaper clipping fluttered to the ground.

Isa quickly scanned the article and felt her heart stretch tight. She slipped the newspaper clipping back into the envelope and stuck it between two books on her bookshelf. Then she left her room and crept down the hall to her parents' room.

Mama was sleeping alone in the bed. Isa got under the covers and curled in next to her.

Mama opened her eyes. "Hi, sweetie," she murmured.

"Mama," Isa said, rubbing her chest where her heart lay underneath. "Everything hurts."

"I know, sweetie," Mama said, stroking her hair. "I know."

When Isa finally drifted off an hour later, the brownstone groaned with relief as the last Vanderbeeker fell into a fitful sleep.

Local Mother and Daughter Killed in Harlem Motorist Accident

Abigail Beiderman, 42, and her daughter, Luciana Beiderman, 16, were crossing the street at 137th Street and Convent Avenue when they were struck by a cab, said police. They were five blocks away from their Harlem home. The driver, David Albertson, sustained minor injuries.

"A cab came speeding around the corner," said Helene Castleman, a local baker, who witnessed the accident in front of her business. "It was a horrible scene."

The victims were rushed to Harlem Hospital, where Abigail Beiderman was pronounced dead. Luciana Beiderman died from injuries later that evening. The driver was released from the hospital, and police are investigating whether he was driving while intoxicated. No arrests have been made.

TUESDAY, DECEMBER 24

Eighteen

Jessie's eyes flew open. It took her a few moments to register her father snoring on the floor and George Washington kneading the blanket draped over her. Paganini hopped circles around Papa and nudged Papa's feet with his nose, ready to start the day. Jessie put her hand on her heart and rubbed.

Today was Christmas Eve.

Papa emitted a powerful snore and woke himself up.

"What? Grab the coats!" he said, bolting upright. He looked around, confused, then saw Jessie staring down at him.

"Oh, hey, sweetie. Sorry about that. Was I snoring?"

"Yes, Papa."

"Did I say weird things in my dreams?"

"Yes, Papa."

They got up, folded the blankets, and started preparing breakfast. Jessie retrieved her list of things to do for Christmas Eve dinner and examined it while listening to the sounds of her family awakening upstairs. Her stomach was full of knots as she waited for Isa to come down.

First Laney appeared, wearing her panda coat and talking to her stuffed bunny about what presents she wanted for Christmas. Oliver stumbled into the kitchen next, his hair in disarray. Jessie felt Oliver's eyes settle on her as she pretended to review the dinner menu.

"Mama is going to help you make dinner, right?" Oliver asked her.

"I don't know." Jessie adjusted her glasses. "Probably not."

"I think she should. It's *Christmas Eve dinner,*" Oliver reminded her, perhaps unwisely.

"I think you should be quiet," Jessie snapped.

Papa spoke up. "Oliver, my beloved son—"

"*Only* son," Jessie grumbled under her breath.

"—this would be a good time to give your sister some space," Papa finished.

Oliver shrugged and tried not to think too hard about what he had said wrong. He knew he would never understand.

Hyacinth came downstairs with Franz at her heels, followed by Mama's light footsteps. At last, Jessie heard the last set of familiar footfalls. Out of the corner of her eye, she watched Isa make her way into the kitchen. Isa picked up Laney and settled her on her hip, greeting everyone except Jessie.

Jessie dared to look up at her sister. "What time do you want to start cooking?" she asked.

"Whenever," Isa replied, avoiding her glance as she kissed Laney's nose and put her down on the floor.

Jessie tapped her pencil against her dinner notes. She felt uncharacteristically apprehensive. "Should we split up the list? I can make the beef stew and the cheesecake. Do you want to do the roasted vegetables and carrot cake?"

"Fine."

"If you'd rather do the beef stew, I can do the roasted vegetables."

"Whatever."

Jessie hesitated. "Does that mean you want to do the beef stew, or do you want to make the roasted vegetables?"

"I don't care." Isa turned away from Jessic to grab a mug from the cupboard.

"So should we stick with the original plan?"

"Fine!" Isa whipped around and glared at Jessie. Then she turned her glare to Oliver and Hyacinth, who had been spectators to the entire exchange, their gazes bouncing back and forth.

"Well!" Hyacinth said to no one in particular. "Looks like Franz wants to visit the kittens in the backyard!" She grabbed a snoozing Franz by the collar and dragged him outside.

Oliver's delivery was equally unbelievable. "Yeah, gotta run. Going to, uh, organize my bookshelves . . ." He trailed off, then scurried up the stairs two at a time.

"Listen," Mama said, one hand braced on Isa's shoulder and the other braced on Jessie's. "We can see that you two are working something out. However, seven hungry adults and three hungry kids are counting on you for dinner tonight. Papa and I will take the kids down the street to help wrap gifts for the toy drive, so we'll be out of your hair. Are you two going to be okay? Should we think about a plan B?"

"We can do it," Isa muttered. Jessie nodded mutely. The day couldn't be over soon enough.

※ ※ ※

An hour later, the Vanderbeekers' home was eerily quiet. While the rest of the family was at PS 737's school cafeteria wrapping gifts for the toy drive, Isa and Jessie went about their dinner preparations without a word, every sound echoing throughout the kitchen.

Jessie retrieved her beef stew ingredients mechanically. Her stomach felt squeamish and unsteady—the last time she had felt like this was when she ate the fish head stew Allegra's mom had made. (*It does amazing things for your kidneys,* Allegra's mom, the pediatrician, had said. *Even if I throw it all up?* Jessie had thought but not said.)

Jessie chopped the onions, carrots, celery, and garlic. Put them in a bowl. Lined up her seasonings. Turned the burner on. Added olive oil to the pot.

Threw in the vegetables, then beef, then broth. Stirred. Waited.

Isa was doing her own chopping on the kitchen counter, her knife pounding against the scarred cutting board. Potatoes, mushrooms, bell peppers, and carrots were all dumped together in a roasting pan with olive oil, salt, and pepper. Isa set the oven to four hundred degrees, shoved the roasting pan inside, and let the oven door bang closed. Then she stomped downstairs to the basement. Soon after, Jessie heard the sounds of Isa's bow striking her violin in a moody rendition of "La Folia."

Jessie collapsed onto a kitchen stool, arms crossed on the counter, head buried in her arms. She stayed there, unmoving, while the steam rattled the lid on the soup pot up and down, up and down.

❋ ❋ ❋

Hyacinth was the first one out of the school when the Vanderbeekers were done with gift wrapping. The second she got home, she leashed up Franz and was back outside before her family had even made it inside.

"Franz-and-I-are-going-to-hang-out-in-the-back-yard-okay-see-you-later-bye!" Hyacinth blurted out. No one questioned her, even though it was thirty-five degrees and the trees lining the sidewalk bent against the strain of the wind.

"Franz, listen up. It's time for our secret spy mission."

First they stopped by the alley where Papa kept the gray trash cans and blue recycling bins. Hyacinth sifted through a stack of boxes Mama had deemed too small to be useful for the move. After choosing the perfect one, Hyacinth and Franz made their way to the hydrangea bush in the corner of the backyard, just beyond the big oak.

Underneath the bush was a family of cats. Hyacinth had been feeding the mama, a sleek black cat she had named Francesca Priscilla Arlington, for the last two months and had salvaged a small wooden cabinet abandoned on the sidewalk for her to live in after she gave birth to her litter six weeks ago. The cabinet was lined with old fuzzy blankets Hyacinth had procured from Miss Josie and Mr. Jeet.

Franz tilted his head and one ear twitched. He stuck

his face inside the cabinet and nuzzled the three kittens, who responded by batting his nose playfully. Hyacinth stroked Francesca Priscilla Arlington and leaned down to kiss her head. For a moment, Hyacinth's resolve faltered. But then—as if her father were right next to her whispering in her ear—Hyacinth remembered something.

Until one has loved an animal, a part of one's soul remains unawakened.

Hyacinth took a deep breath, then lifted the little black kitten with the smudges of white fur on her paws out of the cabinet. "We're going to take real good care of your baby," Hyacinth whispered to Francesca Priscilla Arlington. She placed the kitten in the box, removed her own scarf—a rainbow-colored piece she had knitted herself—and tucked it around the kitten. Kitten and box in hand, Hyacinth led the way out of the alley and back up the brownstone's front stairs. She entered the first-floor hallway, crept along the walls on tiptoe, and looped the end of Franz's leash to the doorknob that led to their apartment. She kissed Franz on his cold nose.

"You must be very, very quiet," she whispered to

him. Franz looked back into her hazel eyes, and Hyacinth knew in her soul that he understood the importance of this moment.

Hyacinth commenced the final stage of her superspy mission. Up she went to the third floor with the box in her arms. Her hands shook when she laid the box in front of the Beiderman's door. She clenched a trembling hand into a fist, paused only slightly, then banged on the door. Down two flights of stairs she flew before grabbing Franz's leash off the door handle and disappearing into her apartment. The sound of her pounding heart so filled her ears that she couldn't tell whether the door on the third floor had opened or not.

Nineteen

The entire Vanderbeeker family was sprawled around the living room when Papa's cell phone rang. He answered it, and the kids abruptly quieted when they heard him say, "Hello, Mr. Beiderman, how are you?" There was a pause, then, "Oh really? The last *two* mornings? I had no idea." Papa cast a you-have-a-lot-of-explaining-to-do look in the kids' direction while Mama leaned in close to the phone.

The Vanderbeeker kids gave each other uneasy glances before backing up in the direction of the stairs.

"I'm very surprised," Papa continued, glaring at his kids. "That doesn't sound like them. You saw them out your window? I see. I will definitely talk with them. That is completely unacceptable, and I'm very sorry."

Papa's glare at his retreating children intensified as

he pointed one stern finger at them, then to a spot on the ground one foot away from him.

"I'm very sorry, Mr. Beiderman. The sudden move has been hard on them. I'm sure you can understand that."

The kids arrived at the designated spot in front of Papa and stared at the ground.

"Yes, of course. We will be out by December thirty-first, maybe earlier. Again, I'm sorry, Mr. Beiderman. I hope you have a happy holi—" Papa stopped and looked down at the phone screen. "The man just hung up on me," Papa muttered. He set his phone on top of a side table, then turned slowly to face the kids.

"Anything you want to tell me?" Papa asked, looking at each of his kids.

No one said anything.

"That was Mr. Beiderman," Papa said. "He told me about a petition that you kids put together. He's very, very upset."

Isa twisted her fingers together. Jessie looked straight ahead at a crack in the brownstone wall. Oliver's eyes darted to each of his siblings in panic. Hyacinth's eyes filled with tears as she reached down to stroke Franz's ears. Laney was the only one looking up at Papa, with glum brown eyes.

"Mr. Beiderman is furious, not only about the petition, but because someone—and from the way he described her, it sounded like it might be your friend Allegra—figured out his phone number and circulated it throughout the neighborhood." The twins grimaced while Papa continued. "People have been calling him all day demanding that he renew our lease. He had to disconnect his phone."

Hyacinth held her breath, waiting for Papa to bring up the kitten, but he didn't.

Oliver spoke up. "We thought it would encourage him to let us stay if he knew how many people loved us in the neighborhood," he explained.

"I know you kids love the brownstone. Your mama and I love it too. But you cannot do things like this. It's hurtful to Mr. Beiderman, and I expect you all to apologize. You will each write him a note and slide it under his door. Please do not disturb him anymore."

"The petition was my idea," Isa said, a flush covering her cheeks. "We didn't know Allegra would have people call him," she added quickly. "I just wanted to show the Beiderman how important this place is to us. I can see how the petition was wrong. I'm sorry. I'm really, really sorry."

Isa looked at her siblings. Hyacinth's face was pale, Laney was openly crying, Jessie was yanking at a loose thread on her T-shirt, and Oliver was grinding the toe of his sneaker into the wooden floor. Isa took a deep breath.

"We have something else to tell you," Isa said. Oliver looked at her in panic and shook his head briskly. Isa glanced away from him. "We did something else . . ."

Papa dropped his head as if he couldn't handle more bad news. Mama sighed and crossed her arms over her chest.

"We sent away a man who came to look at our apartment," Isa said in a whisper.

"I told him he was walking in the wrong direction," Oliver jumped in. "But I didn't feel good about it!"

There was a long pause while Papa and Mama communicated with their eyes. "This is a fine mess," Papa finally said. "Not only are you getting extra chores next week, but you will each write a letter of apology to Mr. Beiderman, *and* you will also confess what you did with the prospective tenant. In person."

"But, Papa," protested Jessie.

"No. No excuses," Mama said. "We're disappointed in you."

"Okay, Papa," said Isa, her voice trembling. "I'll make sure we apologize right." She felt the weight of failure hang heavy on her. Failing to convince the Beiderman that they were worth keeping. Failing to hold on to their home. Failing her parents. Failing, failing, failing.

Papa finally broke the silence. "I know this has been hard on you kids," he said. "I wish I could have . . ." He paused and shook his head, and instead of finishing his sentence, he opened his arms and Isa fell into him, sobs pouring out of her. After a moment, the other kids and Mama gathered in, mourning all the things they could not hold on to.

❖ ❖ ❖

The Vanderbeeker kids headed upstairs to Isa and Jessie's bedroom, where the only sound was the rattle of the windows in their frames from the winter winds.

Isa still refused to look at or speak to Jessie. Hyacinth helped Laney write "I'm sorry. Love, Laney" before writing her own apology letter. Jessie watched Isa slip the CD she had made for the Beiderman into an envelope. When everyone was done, they trudged upstairs. Hyacinth was relieved to see that the kitten and the box were gone.

The Vanderbeeker kids took turns sliding their letters of apology under the door. Oliver pushed through Mr. Rochester's business card last. A sticky note was attached to the card with a hasty scribble on it that said, "He's the right guy for the brownstone."

❋ ❋ ❋

"Who's ready for *Christmas?*"

Auntie Harrigan and Uncle Arthur were waiting in the living room with huge smiles, tinsel draped around their necks and Santa hats on their heads, when the Vanderbeekers returned from their trip to the Beiderman's apartment. Auntie Harrigan had altered her hair again; this time it was dyed bright red and cut super short and spiky. Uncle Arthur had grown a grizzly beard and was wearing a plaid flannel work shirt with paint-splattered jeans. They were holding piles of presents all wrapped decadently in striped paper and abundant ribbons.

The kids tried their best to look happy.

"I must admit," said Auntie Harrigan as she pulled the kids in for a hug, "I'm not used to such glum reactions when you kids see me. Did I forget someone's birthday? Miss an important dance concert or basketball game?"

The kids shook their heads; then, one by one, they told her the story of the Beiderman and the move. Auntie Harrigan, who had already heard about their impending move from Papa, sat herself down on a cardboard box full of packed books and listened to every word. After the kids finished, there was a prolonged period of silence while Auntie Harrigan chewed on her lip, deep in thought. The kids watched her, hoping she might have the perfect solution for them.

Finally, Auntie Harrigan sighed. "I'm sorry, kids. I wish I knew how to help you. But I'm very, very proud of you. I think those nice things you did for Mr. Beiderman were meaningful to him, even if it doesn't seem like it."

The kids nodded, unbelieving.

Auntie Harrigan stood up and clapped her hands. "If it's going to be the last Christmas Eve dinner here, we better make it really, really great. Your mom told me that you ladies"—she smiled at the twins—"are cooking for us tonight! What a treat!"

Oliver mimed gagging motions that everyone ignored.

The twins went back to dinner preparations while Auntie Harrigan taught the other kids how to draw armadillos. Franz, excited about the visitors and the general chaotic state of the apartment, could not keep still. After he drooled on her drawing multiple times, Laney took charge. "Franz, come!" she said sternly, jabbing her finger at the floor next to her.

Franz ignored her—he only answered to Hyacinth. Paganini, however, bolted from his shoebox and skidded to a stop at Laney's feet.

"Good boy!" Laney said to her bunny, thrilled.

Auntie Harrigan's jaw dropped. "Does that bunny know commands?"

Oliver scoffed. "That bunny? His brain is the size of an acorn!"

Laney looked like she was either going to protest or burst into tears, but she was saved from both when Mama entered the living room with an announcement.

"I just got off the phone with Miss Josie," Mama called out. "Change of plans. We're going to gather in their apartment for dinner. We thought it would be easier, given . . ." Mama gestured at the mess of boxes stacked in unstable piles throughout the living room.

Auntie Harrigan accompanied Mama to the second floor to help set up, while Papa and Uncle Arthur carried up a long folding table, followed by a dozen folding chairs. Laney put Paganini in his carrier, detained only briefly by Mama, who unsuccessfully tried to make a case that Paganini would be more comfortable at home. The twins went to their room to change clothes.

When Uncle Arthur came down to retrieve more chairs, he caught Oliver examining the food.

"What's the verdict?" he asked.

Oliver knew Uncle Arthur was referring to Oliver's running tally of the twins' edible versus inedible meals (the twins were currently at a 43 percent success rate).

"I'm scared to try it," Oliver replied, poking at a piece of blackened vegetable.

"C'mon, how bad could it be? When I was little, your grandma made us eat fried rabbit livers with pepper jelly. You kids have it easy. We got blackened vegetables on the good days."

Oliver dipped the ladle into the beef stew. "I won't tell Laney and Hyacinth that you're a rabbit killer if you eat this bite of stew. And no spitting it out." He held the ladle up to his uncle. "Double dog dare."

"Ha!" Uncle Arthur scoffed. "Easiest dare ever." He took the ladle from Oliver and tipped it into his mouth. There was a pause as his mouth adjusted to the taste; then he sprinted to the sink and spit it out. "Salty! Need . . . water," he gasped, gulping water directly from the faucet spout. When he recovered, he turned to Oliver. "You win."

"At least the bread's from Castleman's," Oliver offered.

"Bread and water for dinner," said Uncle Arthur. "How Dickensian."

So much for their last Christmas Eve in the brownstone.

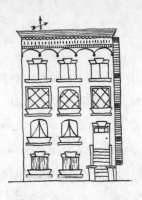

Twenty

Isa and Jessie changed silently in their bedroom and tossed their food-splattered clothes into the laundry hamper. Outside, the wind swooshed and whistled. Isa left the room with her violin in hand, and Jessie found herself alone with her thoughts.

Isa's angry words from the previous day kept running through her head. *Do you have the right to make decisions for me? We are not the same.*

Jessie recalled the tears running down her sister's face at the idea of Benny taking another girl to the dance. Did Isa really like Benny? What if Isa and Benny didn't reconcile before they moved?

Jessie looked around their bedroom. She thought about all the nights they had stayed up late, talking in whispers and using their pillows to muffle their laughter. Jessie saw Isa's perfectly made bed and her own bed with its twisted sheets and rumpled blankets. In the corner of the room by the big window, there was a loose floorboard that the twins had pried up five years earlier when they were convinced that a treasure was hidden underneath. Now they used the space to stash Halloween candy before Mama confiscated it.

Jessie took a deep breath. She couldn't fix the Beiderman problem. She couldn't fix the moving problem. But she could try to fix the Benny problem.

☀ ☀ ☀

Mr. Van Hooten, his violin case slung over his shoulder, blew into the brownstone right before dinner began, exclaiming over the severe weather. He whipped off his hat, revealing a head of unruly hair. He greeted the adults, hugged the kids, and kissed Franz right on the lips.

After numerous runs up and down the stairs to retrieve food and flatware and dishes, the table was finally set. Auntie Harrigan added her own contributions to the table: a glazed ham and a flourless chocolate cake. Miss Josie set out a pot of collard greens and Southern cornbread.

Gloom hung heavy over the dinner table as the kids sat themselves down for their final Christmas Eve dinner in the brownstone. Papa said the blessings and thanked everyone for coming. After a round of applause for the cooks—the twins looking like they were being sentenced to a year's worth of dishwashing—everyone dug in.

Oliver made a point to avoid the beef stew when it was offered to him. He surreptitiously observed everyone else as they scooped large ladlefuls into their bowls. When no one spit it out, Oliver reached across the table to ladle a small amount of the stew into his bowl, then took a tentative sip. But wait! It tasted normal! What happened to all the salt?

Auntie Harrigan nudged his arm and winked. "Amazing what a little extra water and broth can do," she whispered.

"Ahh," Oliver said. He looked over at Uncle Arthur, who saluted Oliver with his soup spoon. "I guess this will bump up their edible meal percentage."

Auntie Harrigan shrugged. "I do what I gotta do," she responded.

A more morose Christmas Eve dinner had never been had among the Vanderbeekers. Every window rattled ominously against the wind, which increased in severity throughout the meal. The adults provided most of the conversation, and the kids offered one-word answers whenever a question was directed at them, with the exception of Laney, who offered a running commentary of every thought that went through her head.

Dinner was not a long affair; no one had an appetite. Finally, Mr. Jeet leaned over and whispered conspiratorially to Laney. When she nodded, Mr. Jeet called for everyone's attention.

"We—have—a—special—treat—for—you," Mr. Jeet announced. "Please—gather—around."

Laney sought out Paganini from under the fronds of a potted palm tree. The jaunty bow tie she had tied around his neck earlier had vanished. Laney lured Paganini out with a few carrot pieces, then led him to the center of the living room.

"And now, grand presenting the famous Paganini!" She gestured to Paganini, who was grooming his ears. The puzzled audience looked at Paganini, unsure why they were doing so.

"We will now demonstrate Paganini's smartness!" Laney announced. Oliver choked on the water he was drinking, and Uncle Arthur pounded on his back.

Laney walked over to the other side of the room, then said, "Paganini, COME!"

Paganini hopped over to Laney and sat up on his hind legs. The audience clapped and nodded in appreciation, impressed that Paganini was not hard of hearing, as previously believed.

"Good boy, Paganini!" Laney exclaimed, giving him a carrot.

"I knew there was something funny going on with that bunny," Auntie Harrigan commented under her breath to Uncle Arthur.

When the applause quieted down, Laney began again. "And now, another trick!" She walked ten feet away from Mr. Jeet, and Paganini followed her. Mr. Jeet held an embroidery hoop one inch off the floor.

"Paganini—HOOP!" Mr. Jeet called out. Paganini zigzagged back over to Mr. Jeet and executed a clean jump through the hoop. Mama's jaw dropped. A slow grin came over Papa's face. Even Oliver was impressed.

When the room quieted, Laney gave another command. "Paganini, lie down!" Paganini flopped on his side, an ear hanging over his eye. The audience cheered.

"Last trick!" said Laney. Mr. Jeet leaned down and placed a toy piano on the floor in front of him.

"Paganini, play piano!" Paganini scrambled up from his prone position and hopped to the piano. Then he placed his front paws on the keyboard and pressed down, creating a discordant chord. And for that moment, the Vanderbeeker kids forgot their troubles and joined the adults in loud applause and cheers. Mr. Jeet and Laney stood up together and held hands, then took a deep bow.

"Encore, encore!" Papa shouted. Jessie took one of the flowers from the vase on the dining room table and tossed it at Laney's feet. When Paganini tried to eat it, Mr. Jeet reached down to rescue the flower and handed it to Laney with a gallant nod. Laney curt-seyed seven times before running to Mama and jumping into her arms.

There was such terrific noise following Paganini's show that at first no one noticed the persistent banging on the ceiling, dull thuds that came in short spurts before starting again.

Mama leaned over to Papa. "Do you hear that noise?"

Papa, who was congratulating Mr. Jeet, paused to listen.

The banging began again. "I think it's coming from upstairs," Mama said uneasily.

Isa's good mood after Laney's bunny performance vanished. She glared at the ceiling as if she could beam lasers from her eyes and decimate the upstairs occupant. One by one, people began to glance upward.

"What's that banging, Papa?" Laney asked.

"I think it's Mr. Beiderman," Miss Josie said apologetically. "He does that sometimes when people come over. I think we get a little . . . loud for him."

Every single person in the room stared at her.

"Did you say Beiderman?" asked Mr. Van Hooten, a peculiar look on his face.

"He bangs on your ceiling?" said Mama, shocked.

"Down with the Beiderman!" shouted Oliver, fist raised high above his head.

Miss Josie lifted her hands helplessly, as if apologizing.

The room buzzed with indignation when the banging resumed, louder than ever.

Isa shot out of her chair. She grabbed her violin from the console next to the front entrance, jerked the door open, and took the stairs two at a time up to the Beiderman's apartment. Isa could vaguely hear her family rush out behind her, but it didn't stop her from pounding a fist on the door.

It opened with a terrific bang, as if the Beiderman had been waiting for Isa to arrive.

"WHAT?" the Beiderman roared. His eyes flashed and he loomed above Isa in his midnight-black clothes. The wind howled around the brownstone.

Isa, her usually tidy hair now an angry halo, pointed the tip of her violin bow one inch from the Beiderman's cold heart.

"You." Isa spoke in a low, dangerous voice. "You are a terrible, grouchy, horrible person. You are mean to Miss Josie and Mr. Jeet. You are making us move for no reason. And now you are ruining our last Christmas here."

Isa pushed the hair off her shoulder and put her violin up, clenched her eyes shut, and crashed her bow onto the strings.

The piece was "Les Furies," and Isa's playing was harsh and unrelenting. It was as if she were dueling against her own fury and disappointment and frustration and loneliness. Around her the brownstone braced itself against the wind and against her rage.

She played because the Beiderman was cruel.

She played because she had disappointed her parents and failed her siblings.

She played because Benny hated her.

She played because they had to move out of the home they loved.

She played because she was fighting with her sister and best friend, the person she loved most in the world.

She played because their mission had failed, and now there was nothing else she could do.

The music exploded through the brownstone, reverberating through the brick walls and making the air crackle. The brownstone shuddered and shook. Outside, the water wall was a frenzy of chimes knocking madly into each other, and the sounds of crashing metal. When it seemed as if the walls themselves would start to crumble, the tension eased. Almost imperceptibly, Isa's violin gentled, as if coaxing "Les Furies" into submission. Then quietly, so quietly, her bow glided along the first note of "The Swan." If "Les Furies" had cleansed her heart of her rage, "The Swan" opened up space for grace to enter in again.

The wind outside eased, and the brownstone groaned with relief.

Isa's bow slowed as she came to the end of the piece, suspended over the last, ethereal high note. The sound continued to ring throughout the brownstone long after the bow had left the violin.

When Isa opened her eyes, she had forgotten where she was. The Beiderman stood in front of her, his face so pale, his skin almost looked translucent. Isa took down her violin and found herself reaching out to touch his arm. The Beiderman stepped back and lifted his head to look at her with miserable, watery eyes.

"I'm sorry," the Beiderman rasped. He gazed at Isa and her violin for another long moment.

Then he closed the door in her face.

Twenty-One

Isa descended the staircase with heavy footsteps while her family and friends watched in silence. But the moment her feet touched the second-floor landing, she found herself embraced from all sides, by Hyacinth and Laney, by Oliver and Mr. Van Hooten, by her parents and Mr. Jeet and Miss Josie and Auntie Harrigan and Uncle Arthur.

"What happened?" yelled Oliver impatiently, pulling at her arm.

"Were you scared, Isa? You saw him, right? He looked like a werewolf, right?" Hyacinth asked, bouncing on the balls of her feet.

"Are you okay, honey?" asked Papa. He cupped Isa's chin in concern.

"That was the most excellent 'Les Furies' I have ever heard," Mr. Van Hooten said, wiping tears from the corners of his eyes. "I wish you would play like that in your lessons."

Miss Josie ushered Isa inside the apartment while Mr. Jeet patted Isa's hand.

The only person who didn't have a word to say or a hug to give was Jessie. In fact, she had disappeared. After looking around the living room, Isa wandered into the kitchen in search of her. A movement out the opened window caught her eye. Isa stuck her head out the window, then climbed onto the fire escape.

"Hi," Jessie said. She was sitting on the first step. The wind and rain had stopped, but fat drops fell onto her head from a tree branch.

"Hi," Isa said, lifting her eyes to look up at the water wall. Pieces of tubing were torn from the wall, and two water wheels and all the wind chimes were missing.

"Damage from the storm," Jessie said, watching Isa survey the destruction.

There was a long pause.

"You were awesome up there," Jessie finally said.

Isa didn't reply.

"Isa, please . . ."

Isa shook her head. "I want to know why you did it."

Jessie swallowed, then stared down at her scuffed sneakers. "I never meant to hurt you. I honestly didn't think you wanted to go to the dance. And when I found out you *did* want to go . . . I don't know. I felt like I was losing you. It scared me even more than moving." She finally looked up.

"Jessie . . ." Isa trailed off before stepping closer to her. "You'll always be stuck with me."

Jessie looked up, her eyes hopeful.

"I'm still upset," Isa informed her. "I don't know if I've forgiven you yet."

"I'll make it up to you," Jessie promised. "I'll cook Tuesday dinners for the next month."

Isa contemplated. Then she shook her head and crossed her arms over her chest. "I've been wronged," she said. "I don't know if I'll ever recover . . ."

"Okay! Fine! I'll clean the bathroom when it's your turn."

"For how long?"

"A month?"

Isa fixed her eyes on a point beyond Jessie's shoulder.

"Fine! Three months!"

Isa finally cracked a tiny smile. "Okay."

"Okay to what?" Jessie asked.

"Okay to everything."

✳ ✳ ✳

Papa cleared his throat. "Please, may I give a toast?" When the room quieted, he lifted his wineglass. "We have loved living here. I cannot imagine better neighbors"—he nodded to Miss Josie and Mr. Jeet—"better family"—then to Auntie Harrigan and Uncle Arthur—"or a better teacher"—and finally to Mr. Van Hooten.

"I have always believed that raising kids means more than just being a good parent and trying to do the right things," Papa went on, his voice beginning to wobble. "It means surrounding your kids with amazing people who can bring science experiments and jam cookies, laughter and joy, and beautiful experiences into their lives. From every part of my being, I want to thank you for giving me and my family the gifts of friendship and love."

Miss Josie cried into a lace handkerchief, and Mr. Jeet hiccupped as tears pooled in his eyes. Mr. Van Hooten blew his nose into a dinner napkin, and Auntie Harrigan wiped her eyes with her sleeve. Uncle Arthur disguised his own tears by picking up Laney and burying his head in her neck.

Isa looked at her siblings. Operation Beiderman had officially failed. But beneath the sadness, her heart felt too big for her body.

"We didn't win over the Beiderman," Isa said, "but this made me realize that home is much more than a place." She smiled at her siblings. "It's good to be a Vanderbeeker, wherever we live."

With the speeches done, Laney ran around distributing hugs and kisses, and soon everyone drifted back to the dining room table, taking another helping of food now that appetites had returned. As people finished off dinner and started in on dessert, Isa cleared the table of dirty dishes and was on her way to the kitchen when Mr. Van Hooten pulled her aside.

"Isa, I must tell you something about Mr. Beiderman."

"What about the Beiderman?" asked Oliver, who was walking by with a piece of chocolate cake as big as the plate it was on.

"Are you talking about the Beiderman?" Jessie called from the kitchen.

"Don't talk about the Beiderman without us!" Hyacinth said, pulling Laney away from the dessert table, where she was sticking her fingers into the carrot cake frosting.

Mr. Van Hooten took the stack of dishes out of Isa's hand and set them on a side table.

"I didn't know . . ." Mr. Van Hooten said, his voice lowering, "that your landlord was Mr. Beiderman."

The kids held their breath.

"I knew him . . . a long time ago," Mr. Van Hooten began. "I didn't even remember that this was the building he lived in . . ." He stopped abruptly.

"We know about his wife and daughter," Isa said. "About the car accident."

"What car accident?" Jessie and Oliver and Hyacinth and Laney said at the same time.

"Mrs. Castleman gave me a newspaper article about it," Isa said. "They died in a car accident."

Mr. Van Hooten breathed a sigh of relief. "So you know about that. But what you might not know is that his daughter, Luciana, was a violinist. She was my student."

"A violinist?" the kids echoed.

"She was very talented. Isa, you have always reminded me a little of Luciana. Especially when you were younger."

"Creepy," breathed Jessie. The kids nodded in agreement.

"Well, I wanted to tell you that the violin you've been playing . . . you know it's been in my family for many generations, right? Well, I had lent Luciana that violin too. But then, when she died . . ." Mr. Van Hooten paused. "Well, her father didn't want anything around that reminded him of his daughter, so he returned it. It's been sitting in my closet, shut away . . . until you came along."

Isa let out a breath she didn't know she was holding.

"I thought you should know."

Mr. Van Hooten's voice sounded as though it were coming from far away, as though he were talking to her from the other end of a long tunnel. The Beiderman's daughter. Mr. Van Hooten's violin. Isa's violin. *Luciana's violin.* Luciana touching the same wood, feeling the same vibrations, hearing the same sounds.

And just like that, the story clicked together.

✸ ✸ ✸

When the last of the guests had gone and Miss Josie and Mr. Jeet's apartment was returned to its original condition, Mama and Papa gathered the children and ushered them downstairs to get ready for bed.

Isa changed into her pajamas before heading to the bathroom to brush her teeth. Jessie and Oliver were already there, and Oliver mumbled something with a mouth full of frothy toothpaste.

"What did you say?" Isa asked.

Oliver spit.

"I feel sorry for the Beiderman," Oliver repeated.

"I never thought I would say this, but I feel sorry for him too," Jessie said, rinsing her toothbrush under the faucet.

"I wish you could have seen his face when I went up there," Isa said as she squeezed toothpaste onto her toothbrush. "When he opened the door, his face was all red from yelling and being mad, but when I finished playing 'The Swan,' his face had turned so white. I've never seen anyone look like that before. Like he had seen a ghost."

Oliver rinsed his mouth. "He sort of did see a ghost. The ghost of Luciana." He shook his head. "Geez, that's so creepy."

"That's too weird that she played violin with Mr. Van Hooten too," Isa said. "With the exact same violin. Did you know that violin has a different sound from other violins? The wood is so old it makes this really beautiful ringing sound. The Beiderman *must* have recognized the violin. When Mr. Van Hooten said the Beiderman didn't want anything that reminded him of his daughter, I felt this chill. Now I feel terrible going up there and playing the same violin his daughter did, right in his face. Like I was throwing all these bad memories at him."

Jessie put her arms around Isa and Oliver. "You didn't know. Anyway, it's probably best we're leaving so he can have some peace. I spent so much time avoiding him, and now all I want to do is make him feel better."

"Me too," Isa said.

"Me too," echoed Oliver.

❖ ❖ ❖

Not too much later, the twins were alone in their bedroom, snuggled under their thick comforters.

"I guess this is it," Isa said. "The last Christmas Eve in the brownstone."

The pipes that carried heat to the radiators banged restlessly within the walls.

"Do you think we should do anything else for the Beiderman? Now that we know . . ." Jessie trailed off.

Isa looked over at her violin sitting on her desk. "I think the only thing we can do now is give him what he's wanted all this time: peace."

"I keep thinking about how he lost his whole family in one night," Jessie murmured from her burrow beneath the blankets. "I can't stop thinking about it."

Isa reached over to turn off the lamp next to her bed. Darkness took over the room. "Me too."

"Good night, Isa."

"Good night, Jessie."

Isa lay back on her bed and gazed at the familiar sights. There was the crack in the shape of Eastern Europe on the ceiling. There was the light that fell in a long rectangle onto the floor between their beds from the street lamp right outside their window. There was the warm air from the radiator making the right side of her comforter toasty and cozy. There was the whoosh of a car heading down the street.

There was Jessie, her breathing becoming steady and deep as she drifted off to sleep.

There were the rough grooves of the bricks lining the wall behind her headboard.

There was the whistling of the pipes in the walls of the brownstone; there was the sound of her parents' low murmuring as they climbed the stairs and quietly peeked into the kids' bedrooms; there was the sound of a distant car alarm and a dog's bark.

This was home, and soon there would be goodbye.

WEDNESDAY, DECEMBER 25

Twenty-Two

Oliver was the first to wake up. He had never out-grown the habit of getting up early to scope out the gift situation under the tree on Christmas morning.

He crept downstairs—avoiding the squeaky step—and glanced at Papa, who was snoring on the couch, to which he had been displaced since Uncle Arthur and Auntie Harrigan had taken his room and Mama had bunked with Laney and Hyacinth. Satisfied that Papa was sound asleep, Oliver searched under the tree for gift tags that had his name. There was a compact, heavy box from his parents, which he assumed was a boxed set of books, hopefully the Lord of the Rings trilogy (plus *The Hobbit*). There was a gift from his twin sisters, plus a paper-thin one from Laney. A lumpy present from Hyacinth was tied prettily in one of her much adored ribbons.

Oliver looked at the presents from his family and a strange feeling settled over him. It was a newish feeling; he had felt it the day before when Papa had scolded him and his sisters for the way they had treated the Beiderman. He looked at his offerings: hand sanitizer and rubber bands and an old piece of candy all wrapped messily in tired newsprint. He hardly felt proud of them, nothing like the books his parents had chosen for him or the bizarre knitting he was sure Hyacinth had spent hours working on. Those presents had love in them. His presents had . . . well, nothing.

Oliver scooped up the presents he had planned to give and ran upstairs to his bedroom. He dumped the gifts in the trash, took out six pieces of paper, and started to write.

✤   ✤   ✤

On Christmas morning, Jessie opened her eyes and was relieved to find herself in her own bed, in her own room. Across the room, Isa stirred.

"Oh, hey," Isa said in her groggy I-just-woke-up voice. "What's up?"

"It's Christmas morning," said Jessie. On cue, they heard Hyacinth and Laney burst out of their room and run giggling down the stairs followed by Mama's steady footsteps, to where Papa woke abruptly on the couch, yelling, "Down with foxes and meerkats!" Franz followed suit a few seconds later, his claws clicking on the wooden steps as he raced downstairs to see why there was a commotion that he was not yet a part of.

The twins heard little feet run up the stairs and then up and down the hallway. "It's Christmas, it's Christmas! Time for presents!" yelled Laney as she bounced down the stairs again.

The twins shrugged on hoodies and ran into Oliver, who was leaving his bedroom at the same time.

"What's that?" Isa asked, pointing at the envelopes in his hand.

"You'll see," he said cryptically.

Downstairs they found Laney yanking on Mama's arm, begging her to let them open presents before breakfast. Hyacinth sat by the tree, adding flourishes to her gift wrapping.

"Might as well open the family presents now," Mama relented. "We'll let Auntie Harrigan and Uncle Arthur sleep past six thirty."

The Vanderbeekers surrounded the tree.

"I'd like to give out my presents first," Oliver announced.

The family was speechless. Oliver, in the whole entire history of his life, had never offered to give out his presents first. He passed out the mysterious envelopes while his family watched him in stunned amazement.

Hyacinth was the first to open hers. "'Coupon good for half an hour of button exploration,'" Hyacinth read. She tackled Oliver in jubilation, too overwhelmed to say thank you. After he detangled himself from her, he pulled three heart-shaped buttons from his pocket and handed them over. Hyacinth was rendered mute, which Oliver took as a positive sign.

Laney needed help reading her card. Isa looked at it and read, "'Coupon good for reading five books aloud.'" Laney beamed her brightest smile, and Oliver felt that reading aloud to her wouldn't be as bad as he had thought . . . as long as they were short books.

Isa and Jessie looked at their cards. "'Oliver will not make fun of Isa and Jessie's cooking for one month,'" Isa read. The twins were surprised; everyone knew *that* would be a big sacrifice on his part.

Oliver shrugged. "I think that'll be the hardest one."

Mama's coupon said "One morning volunteering at soup kitchen," and Papa's coupon said "Help Papa mow the lawn one time." The look of pride on their faces made Oliver feel itchy.

"Okay, so what did you all get me?" Oliver said, breaking the moment and reaching for the presents he already knew were his.

Together the family unwrapped the rest of the presents and exclaimed over each one. Oliver got his Lord of the Rings trilogy (plus *The Hobbit*), Jessie received a just-released science encyclopedia that easily outweighed Franz, Isa and Laney got matching panda mittens ("I'll never give these up, never ever ever!" Laney declared), and Hyacinth got a new set of wool yarns in a rainbow of colors.

Papa was surprised to open his gift from Mama and find a brand-new pair of navy-blue coveralls.

"I'm sure you'll need plenty of fix-it mojo wherever we live," Mama said. Papa gave her a tender kiss on the cheek and put the coveralls on right over his pajamas.

Hyacinth saved her special present for Oliver until the very end. When it was time, she stood in front of him and held out a shoebox encrusted with plastic gemstones. He stared at it with no small amount of trepidation before lifting the top. He pulled out a midnight-blue hat long enough to go from his head to his waist. The very tip of the hat was knitted with a fluorescent yellow yarn.

"Did you run out of blue or something?" Oliver asked, lifting up the yellow end.

"That's exactly what happened!" Hyacinth exclaimed.

The whole family held their breath to see his reaction. He glanced again at Hyacinth, then pulled the hat on his head.

"Thanks, Hyacinth," Oliver said with a satisfied grin. "I've actually always wanted a hat like this."

The family gave a collective sigh of relief, and Hyacinth beamed with pleasure. Then the kids gathered together to give out the last present.

Laney held out a thin box to her parents. Mama had preemptive tears in her eyes when she took it, peeled back the tape, and opened up the paper, careful not to tear the wrapping. Nestled inside was a framed photograph of the wall drawing Oliver had made of the family when he was little. It had been printed to be the exact same dimensions as the actual wall drawing. Tears rolled down her face as she lifted it from the box to show to Papa.

"This is . . . perfect," she managed to say.

"We'll hang it in the same location in our new bedroom," Papa promised.

"Nailed the parent presents," Oliver said with a grin. He jogged around like Rocky Balboa and gave his siblings high fives.

❋ ❋ ❋

After the excitement of the Christmas gifts, it was time to get breakfast ready. Laney and Hyacinth headed toward the kitchen, ready to help make pancakes.

While the twins cleaned up the living room, the doorbell rang. Franz skidded to the door, his tail beating the air at 250 wpm.

Isa shoved Franz aside and looked through the peephole. To her surprise, she saw the top of a head that looked suspiciously like the top of Benny's head. She unbolted the door and opened it a crack. It *was* Benny's head. He looked up when the door opened, smiling a hesitant, shy smile.

"Benny?" Isa asked.

"Hey. What's going on?"

Isa glanced at her watch. "It's seven thirty on Christmas Day. What are you doing here?"

"I was just, you know, taking a walk. Saw your place, thought I'd stop by and say hi. You know, wish you all a Merry Christmas . . ." Benny trailed off. Behind Isa, Jessie gestured wildly to Benny and he looked at her in despair.

"I better go help with the pancakes!" Jessie declared, heading to the kitchen, where four pairs of curious eyes blatantly spied on Isa and Benny.

"It's really nice of you to stop by," Isa said to Benny. "Although—aren't your parents wondering where you are?"

"No, I told them I was coming by to say hi to you. They sent this." Benny thrust a bag overflowing with various sweet breads and Christmas cookies at Isa.

Isa took the bag. "Wow! Tell them thanks! Do you want to have breakfast with us?"

Benny glanced at Isa's parents, then back at Isa. "Hey, can we take a walk or something?"

Isa blinked. "A walk? Right now?"

"Yeah. Please?"

"Let me see." Isa turned around to ask her parents, but they were nodding before she even opened her mouth.

"Stay on the block and be back within fifteen minutes, please," Papa said.

Isa nodded, grabbed her jacket, and followed Benny outside.

They walked halfway down the block in silence before Benny mumbled something. Isa glanced at him. Was his face bright red? She leaned toward him. "What did you say?"

Benny looked at Isa, his face definitely fiery red. "I said you look pretty this morning."

Isa looked down at her outfit: beat-up Chuck Taylors, faded fleece pajama pants with music notes on them, fleece hoodie, and puffy winter jacket. She tilted her head. "Are you okay, Benny?" she asked.

"It's true!" Benny said defensively. "I've always thought you were the prettiest girl I know."

Isa's face quickly matched Benny's in color, and after a few minutes of quiet, Benny stopped in the middle of the sidewalk. When Isa realized he wasn't next to her, she stopped and turned around to face him.

"Isa, I'm really sorry for what I said. Jessie called me yesterday and confessed that she had never told you what happened. I'm sorry I assumed you knew about it. I never asked another girl to the dance. I don't even know why I said that. I guess I was . . . embarrassed. I'm really, really sorry."

"Oh, Benny, I'm sorry too. I would never want to hurt your feelings. You are one of my most important friends. I was so upset when you weren't talking to me."

"Since your sister's phone call, I've been waiting and waiting to come and talk to you in person. I wanted to come last night, but Jessie said that you guys were doing a big dinner and that you were still mad at her. So I came as early as I could today. I needed to ask you something in person."

Isa's heart stuttered as Benny took a deep breath.

"Isa, I'd really like for you to go with me to the eighth grade dance next month. Please, will you come with me?"

A slight breeze set a pile of feather-light leaves dancing and rolling down the sidewalk. Benny's shuffling feet rolled against tiny bits of gravel, the sound echoing in her ears.

Years later, her memory would linger on this exact moment. The leaves swirling, the gravel crunching, the crisp smell of winter. But most of all, she would remember Benny's face, so uncertain, and always so dear to her.

✸ ✸ ✸

When Isa and Benny returned to the brownstone, Isa's parents' noses were pressed against the window. They waved as if spying on people on the street were a completely normal part of their morning. Isa gestured for them to come out, and they both acquiesced without bothering to put on jackets.

"Oh, hey, Benny. So nice to see you," Papa said casually. He still wore his new coveralls, his pajamas poking out underneath.

"Hi, Mr. Vanderbeeker. Hi, Mrs. Vanderbeeker," Benny replied.

"Well!" said Mama, rubbing her arms and shivering. "What an interesting morning. Benny, are you joining us for breakfast? Just so you know, the pancakes Hyacinth and Laney made are a complete disaster. Stick with the stuff your parents baked. Do you want to ask them to join us?"

Benny considered this for about half a second. "I'll run over and get them." He loped off and the Vanderbeekers watched him disappear down the street. Frigid from standing outside with no jackets, Mama and Papa ushered Isa inside.

Isa found Jessie setting the table and pulled her into a big hug. "Thank you," Isa whispered.

Jessie nodded. "Does that mean I'm off the hook with cleaning the bathroom?"

"Nope," Isa replied. "But you are officially and totally forgiven."

Jessie considered. "I'll take it," she said.

Hyacinth and Laney were busy setting the table, Franz in their wake. A wobbly stack of pancakes that looked like extraterrestrial spaceships sat in the middle of the table, along with a platter holding the breads the Castlemans had sent over and a clay bowl filled with clementines.

"Woof!" announced Franz, pawing at Hyacinth's feet.

"Franz, you know that pancakes are *not* a part of your diet," Hyacinth scolded as she circled the table laying out utensils.

Franz continued to follow her and whimper, but Hyacinth avoided him.

"Franz, please! I'm trying to set the table!"

Franz howled, then grabbed a corner of Hyacinth's dress gently in his mouth and pulled her toward the stairs. Hyacinth was so surprised by Franz's strange behavior she let herself be pulled. All the way upstairs they went, and when they got to the top, Franz bypassed the bedrooms, snuffled urgently, and pawed the door that led into the building hallway.

"What is it, Franz?" Hyacinth asked him. She pushed him aside and opened the door to find an open packing box on the doormat. Franz stuck his head over the top of the box and licked the forehead of the very same black kitten with white smudged feet they had left on the Beiderman's doorstep the day before. The cat had a ribbon tied around its neck. When Hyacinth took a closer look, she discovered that it was the same green velvet ribbon she had tied around the placemat she had made for the Beiderman.

Strung on the ribbon was a tiny piece of paper. Hyacinth untied the ribbon from the kitten's neck and peered at the note.

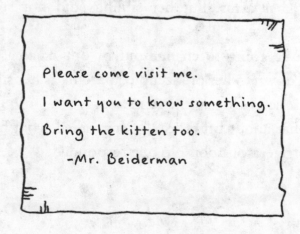

Please come visit me.
I want you to know something.
Bring the kitten too.
    —Mr. Beiderman

Twenty-Three

Hyacinth tucked the kitten against her chest and sprinted inside with Franz close behind. Down the stairs she tumbled, seeking out each of her siblings and whispering, "Family meeting, NOW!" Maybe it was the crazed look in Hyacinth's eyes, or the fact that she was cradling a strange yet adorable kitten in her arms, but her siblings did not stop to argue.

"We're going to change out of our pajamas!" Isa called down to her preoccupied parents as her siblings made a hasty exit up the stairs.

"What about breakfast?" Papa called from behind the refrigerator door. No one responded.

Hyacinth led her siblings out the first-floor exit into the main hallway of the brownstone, where the stairs rose to the other two apartments.

"Look what I found attached to the kitten I gave to the Beiderman," Hyacinth said. She handed Oliver the card.

"You gave the Beiderman this kitten? Why on earth would you do that?" asked Jessie, her eyes wide.

"Shush," Isa said to Jessie. Then she ordered Oliver to read the card.

Oliver read it out loud, then started pacing back and forth. "Oh man, oh man. What do you think he wants?"

Before anyone could answer, Isa caught sight of Laney. The littlest Vanderbeeker had taken it upon herself to go up the stairs, and she was already halfway between the second and third floors.

"Laney!" they called, stumbling upstairs after her. But it was too late. She was pounding cheerfully on the door and calling out, "Mr. Beezleman! We're here! We have your kitten!"

By the time the other kids caught up with her, the

locks were already disengaging. The door opened, and the Beiderman looked down on them. Hyacinth's first thought was that he didn't look half as werewolfish as he had when she'd dropped off the placemat. Her second thought was *I feel brave.*

"Come in." The Beiderman stepped back and gestured inside. He wore black, but his hair was combed neatly and he had shaved his beard. For a moment, no one moved. Then the kitten executed a graceful leap out of Hyacinth's arms and trotted inside, the tip of her tail flicking behind her.

"Please," the Beiderman said. "Please come in."

Hyacinth stood up straight, channeling Hyacinth the Brave, and stepped inside with Franz at her heels. Oliver followed, his new blue knit hat with the fluorescent yellow tip trailing down his back. Laney entered next, followed by Jessie and Isa.

Violin music was playing softly from a stereo in the corner. Isa's eyes widened when she realized it was the CD she had made for him of her own playing. The apartment was sparse; there was a dining room table for one with a chair tucked into it, a worn sofa, a crooked side table, and two standing floor lamps.

The Christmas tree Laney had picked out was displayed in the middle of the table, right in front of the placemat Hyacinth had made. Laney's picture of the brownstone was taped to the wall next to Hyacinth's wreath. The science project Jessie had made was resting on the side table next to the sofa where Oliver's letter and his haiku lay on the armrest. It was all there.

But what the kids noticed more than the gifts they had given him were the many, many paintings; large and small, all black and white, and on every available wall space. The paintings showed a girl of different ages, from newborn to teenager, sometimes alone on the canvas and other times with a woman that looked their mom's age. Other canvases depicted just the woman. Some paintings were stark, as if the brush had crashed and torn against the canvas, while other paintings were tender, as if they had been painted over the course of hundreds of hours with the tip of the thinnest brush.

The kids settled their eyes back on the Beiderman.

He had not moved from his position by the door, and the black kitten was winding itself around his ankles and mewling.

The Beiderman, with the force of the kids' stares on him, cleared his throat. "I'm Mr. Beiderman," he said, somewhat unnecessarily, his voice rough. The kids looked back at him uneasily. "I'm sorry for"—the Beiderman coughed, then paused and waved one hand—"everything."

None of the kids said anything. The Beiderman looked at Isa, then away again. Then he looked back at her. "I'm sorry. About last night. About not renewing your lease. It's just that—" Mr. Beiderman stuttered to a stop.

"It's okay, Mr. Beiderman," said Isa. "We know. We're sorry about your family."

Mr. Beiderman swallowed. "A few months ago," he said to Isa, "you played Luciana's favorite song outside on the brownstone steps. It was too much for me. I thought it would be easier . . ." He trailed off, not finishing the sentence.

They stood there in silence. The only sound was the brownstone floors creaking when the kids shifted.

Then Hyacinth spoke up. "Did you make all those paintings?"

He nodded.

"You must miss them so much."

Mr. Beiderman looked at her. "I miss them every second of every day."

Isa felt her heart pounding in her chest. "Mr. Beiderman," she said, "we would like to be your friends. That is, if it's not too hard to be with us."

Laney walked over to her neighbor, and, without hesitation, she hugged him as only a four-and-three-quarters-year-old can hug.

"Let's be friends," she said, her voice muffled against him. Mr. Beiderman looked down at her in surprise, his face filled with both despair and longing. When Laney detached herself, he kneeled down. He didn't respond, but he reached for her hand.

Mr. Beiderman glanced up at Oliver.

"I'm sorry," Oliver said, stepping forward. "For the awful note."

Mr. Beiderman nodded. "I deserved it, and more."

Hyacinth took Mr. Beiderman's hand and pulled him up. "Come on, it's time for Christmas breakfast."

"Oh no, I can't go," said Mr. Beiderman as he resisted Hyacinth. "I can't leave this apartment."

"You left to bring the kitten with the note down," said Jessie matter-of-factly.

"That was the one and only time," he replied.

"Not the only time," said Isa, helping Hyacinth lead him out the door. "The first of many."

❀ ❀ ❀

Mama and Papa were waiting at the bottom of the apartment stairs by the kitchen when the kids came back to the apartment.

"What on earth were you doing up there for so long?" Mama cried as the kids descended the staircase. "And how come you're still in your pajamas?"

"We can explain," said Jessie.

But Mama was on a roll. "The Castlemans have been here for ten minutes! Even Auntie Harrigan and Uncle Arthur are awake!"

Isa appeared, leading a hesitant Mr. Beiderman down the stairs. "Mama, we'd like to introduce you to Mr. Beiderman."

Mama and Papa gaped as Mr. Beiderman emerged from behind the children. He maneuvered around the moving boxes stacked along the banister.

"I'm so sorry to intrude," he said in a voice so quiet they all strained to hear him. "I was manhandled."

Papa recovered first. "No, no," he said weakly. "Please, come in. Um, Merry Christmas." He gestured vaguely to the Castlemans. "Do you know the Castlemans?"

"Hello," Mr. Beiderman said.

"Hello," they echoed back.

Isa looked at her mother. "Mama, can we get Mr. Beiderman something to eat?"

"Oh yes!" Mama came out of her trance and bustled around, grabbing many bread items and placing them on a plate in an overflowing heap. She pushed it into Mr. Beiderman's arms, then asked, "Coffee? Tea? Milk? Juice? Flat water? Sparkling water?"

Hyacinth slipped in. "Mama, we'll get him a drink. You help the Castlemans." The Castlemans were now in hushed conversation with Auntie Harrigan and did not look as if they needed assistance, but Mama raced over there anyway.

"Can I get you something to drink, Mr. Beiderman?" Hyacinth asked. Her siblings hovered around Mr. Beiderman protectively.

"Water. Please," Mr. Beiderman said faintly. She disappeared to the kitchen and returned with a glass of water. He took a sip, then looked at the Vanderbeeker kids. "Even after I've been so terrible to you, you still want to live in the same building as me?"

The Vanderbeeker kids did not even dare to breathe as they nodded. Mr. Beiderman swallowed.

"I would like you to stay living here, in the brownstone," he said, then added hastily, "if you would still like to."

There was a brief pause, then joy burst forth and rang throughout the brownstone. Laney and Hyacinth jumped up and down and cheered, while Oliver pumped his arms in the air and shouted. Jessie and Isa threw their arms around each other.

Mama and Papa hurried over. "What on earth!" exclaimed Mama.

"We can stay, we can stay!" chanted Hyacinth.

"We don't have to move to Ottenville!" yelled Oliver.

"I get to keep Mr. Van Hooten as my violin teacher!" exclaimed Isa.

Mama and Papa looked wide-eyed at Mr. Beiderman.

"Please. I'd like you and your family to stay in the brownstone," Mr. Beiderman said.

There was stunned silence, then: "Oh, thank you, thank you!" cried Mama, enveloping him in a spontaneous hug. Oliver was afraid Mama would lift him off the ground in her enthusiasm.

"Okay, okay," said Papa, detaching Mama from Mr. Beiderman's neck. Then he put out his hand and shook Mr. Beiderman's. "Thank you. This means so much to us."

"Will you visit me and play the violin?" Mr. Beiderman asked Isa.

"Yes," she replied. "If it's not too hard for you. Mr. Van Hooten told me about the violin."

Mr. Beiderman nodded. "It was nice to see it, to hear it sing again."

He turned to Hyacinth. "Will you teach me how to take care of a cat?"

"Oh yes!" cried Hyacinth.

"I'll help too!" said Laney.

"Laney, can you help me name it?" asked Mr. Beiderman.

"Fluffy," Laney said promptly. "Or Cutie. Or Princess Cutie."

"Let's think about it some more," suggested Mr. Beiderman.

At that moment Miss Josie and Mr. Jeet entered the apartment, and the kids rushed over to share the news.

"We're staying, we're staying!" cried Hyacinth.

Laney grabbed Miss Josie around the waist. "We can be together forever!"

Oliver saw Mr. Jeet smile so big, it looked like someone had told him he'd won a million dollars.

"Is it true?" Miss Josie said, bracing herself on Mrs. Vanderbeeker's arm.

"Yes! Have you met Mr. Beiderman?" asked Mama. She dragged Miss Josie and Mr. Jeet to Mr. Beiderman and bustled off to get food for the new arrivals.

The doorbell rang, and in came Angie and her dad to say goodbye, only to realize that goodbyes were no longer necessary. Mr. Smiley got on his phone to notify the neighbors, and soon enough a crowd of happy friends arrived at the Vanderbeekers' doorstep to celebrate.

When Allegra flew in decked in a flowing red dress with a wide black ribbon tied around her waist, the first thing she did was embrace Isa and exclaim, "Now we *have* to find a guy to take you to the eighth grade dance!"

"Already done," Isa said, smiling at Benny.

"Shut. Up." Allegra looked like she had just been given an early birthday present. "That is so, *so* awesome! I can't wait to tell Carlson. Benny, you better get Isa a corsage. Listen, at the florist on Lenox Avenue, they have this carnation color called amaranth pink. That's the color you need to get, because it will go best with the color of her dress and her hair. Don't forget, *am-uh-ranth* pink. Oh, and you need to wear a suit, okay? No football jerseys allowed."

Benny looked down at his current outfit, a jersey and jeans. Then he looked at Isa in alarm.

But Allegra wasn't done with Benny. "Do you have a friend who can take Jessie?"

"Never going to happen," Jessie said, flicking the remains of her chocolate croissant at Allegra and hitting her right in the middle of the forehead.

A crowd of neighbors, including Mr. Jones the postman and Mr. Ritchie the Christmas tree guy, stopped in, along with Mr. Van Hooten, who pulled out his violin and started playing holiday music. The Vanderbeeker home was filled to capacity with neighbors and friends, all swarming in to congratulate and celebrate.

Mr. Beiderman, in the meantime, spent most of his time sitting on a stool in a sheltered corner of the kitchen, a location that granted him a perfect view of all the happenings around him but protected him from the crush of people. Next to him was Oliver, immersed in his new books. Mr. Beiderman's cat, who Laney had already started calling Princess Cutie, was wrapping herself around his ankles. Isa, Jessie, and their friends stood in a group, laughing about who knows what. Franz turned in circles, attempting to remove a piece of red fabric tied in a jaunty bow around his neck. Laney crawled around the floor, traversing a path that made sense only to her. Uncle Arthur examined the hole in the ceiling that Papa had made during the Great Plumbing Accident, shaking his head in disbelief. Mama and Papa stood in the kitchen, washing dishes, filling glasses, and forcing more food onto their guests' plates. Mr. Beiderman quietly surveyed the scene, and then he took a deep breath. Oliver, who had glanced over at just that moment, said later that it looked like Mr. Beiderman was breathing happiness into his body.

It was hours before the Vanderbeeker apartment cleared out. Mr. Beiderman was one of the first to leave, but only after Laney made him promise to come back the following day for dinner. He cradled his black kitten in his arms as he said a brief goodbye and escaped up to his apartment. The other guests trickled away, until only Auntie Harrigan and Uncle Arthur were left. While Mama and Papa began cleaning up the apartment, the kids helped their aunt and uncle pack up. After innumerable hugs and kisses, Auntie Harrigan and Uncle Arthur got in their car and honked as they rolled down the street while the kids waved and shouted their goodbyes and I-love-yous.

When the car rounded the corner and disappeared from sight, the Vanderbeekers turned and faced the brownstone.

"I guess we should help clean up and start unpacking," Jessie commented.

"Let's start now," Oliver suggested. "I'm ready."

Isa held up a hand. "Let's just ... wait a second." The kids stilled and drank in the sight of the brownstone. The twisting iron fence that surrounded it, the smooth red rock that made up the façade, the wide windows that winked in the sunlight.

When they'd had their fill, the Vanderbeekers filed inside. The brownstone creaked as it settled more firmly into its foundation, wrapping the kids in warmth and love just as it had for so many years past and would, now, for many years to come.

Epilogue

One Month, Six Days Later

A baby blue Volkswagen rattled down West 141st Street and slowed to a stop in front of the red brownstone. The back passenger door opened, and out stepped a gangly eighth grade boy. He was wearing a crisply pressed black suit with a burgundy tie. His hair was still slightly damp and had signs of a recent combing. On his feet were the same sneakers he usually wore when he played basketball. In his hand was a plastic container with an amaranth-pink corsage nestled inside.

He raced up to the front door, then paused before lifting his hand to press the doorbell.

"Hey! Hey, you!" Startled, Benny dropped his hand from the buzzer and looked up. Mr. Beiderman was hanging out his window.

Benny stepped back to get a better vantage point. "Oh. Hey, Mr. Beiderman. It's just me. Benny."

Mr. Beiderman leaned even farther out his window. "I *know* who you are. What are you doing here at this hour?"

"Sir? I'm here to pick up Isa? For the dance?" Benny shivered in the cold. It was late January, and icicles hung from the brownstone eaves. He wanted to make a good first impression when Isa first saw him, so he'd left his coat in the car. He hadn't expected to be standing outside so long.

Mr. Beiderman glared at Benny. "Don't try any funny stuff with Isa. Remember, I have all the time in the world to make your life miserable."

Benny glanced around for hidden hit men, but thankfully, at just that moment, the Vanderbeekers' door flew open and out tumbled Isa. She looked as if she had stepped out of a glossy magazine. She ran right up to Benny and hugged him.

"So much for a grand entrance," Auntie Harrigan remarked, standing in the doorway holding a can of hairspray.

"Move, Harrigan!" Mama said, trying to reach around Auntie Harrigan to snap photos of Isa on her phone.

Papa pushed his way through with Isa's coat. When he saw Benny holding Isa's hand, he scowled. "Rule number one. No touching." Benny dropped Isa's hand. Papa handed Isa her coat.

Uncle Arthur followed Papa outside. He was holding Oliver's plastic pirate sword. "Don't give me a reason to use this on you, boy."

Mama and Isa sighed. From above, Mr. Beiderman coughed. Papa and Uncle Arthur glanced up, and Mr. Beiderman gave them a discreet thumbs-up.

"Hi, Benny!" Jessie called from the roof. Everyone looked up. "Ready for some music?" Jessie disappeared, and soon the chimes and bells of a newly installed water wall rang through the neighborhood.

Oliver launched himself outside. "Hey, Benny. Cool shoes."

Laney, already in her pajamas, made her way outside to see Benny. "Can we see the flower bracelet?"

Franz bounded out next, 320 wpm, with Hyacinth close behind. Benny opened the box and pulled out the corsage, then slipped it around Isa's wrist.

"Ooh," said Hyacinth and Laney.

A window on the second floor creaked open.

"Is it time for the dance?" called Miss Josie. Next to her, Mr. Jeet pushed his head out the window to look down at the crowd.

"It's time!" Isa called up. She grabbed Benny's hand. Papa, Uncle Arthur, and Mr. Beiderman scowled at them again. "We better get going. Poor Benny has no jacket!"

"Let me just get one photo!" called Mama. Isa looked at Benny apologetically; then they moved together to pose for a photo. "Smile!" Mama said, clicking the button at least eleven times before Papa confiscated her phone. Isa and Benny waved and ran to the car, piling into the back seat. From the front seats, Mr. and Mrs. Castleman waved.

"Be careful!" said Papa.

"Bring me back something!" cried Laney.

"Where'd you get your shoes?" Oliver asked Benny.

"I'll wait up for you!" called Jessie from the roof.

"Don't they look lovely?" Miss Josie asked Mr. Jeet.

"I want to make a corsage for myself," said Hyacinth.

"Curfew is at ten o'clock sharp!" Mr. Beiderman yelled at Benny.

"See you back at home! Have fun!" said Mama.

Benny and Isa smiled and waved at everyone, then shut the car door. Slowly, the Castlemans pulled away from the curb.

Mr. Beiderman gave a gruff wave and retreated into his apartment. Miss Josie and Mr. Jeet blew kisses to the Vanderbeekers and closed their windows. Jessie disappeared, and the Vanderbeekers could hear the fire escape creaking as she descended the metal stairs.

The weathervane on top of the brownstone whirled in jubilation as the Vanderbeekers filed back into their home. A home that was, and always would be, the brownstone on 141st Street.

Acknowledgments

This book has been a journey, and I am so grateful for my many fellow travelers. First of all, Ann Rider. I cannot imagine a more perfect editor for me and for this book. I am ever thankful for her gentle nudging and invaluable feedback and for loving the Vanderbeeker kids and giving them a home at HMH. Thank you to the HMH design team, especially Sheila Smallwood, for the gorgeous layout and careful attention to every detail. So many people at HMH have made this book possible, including Mary Wilcox, Lily Kessinger, Karen Walsh, Lisa DiSarro, Mary Magrisso, Tara Shanahan, and Lauren Cepero. I owe so much to Colleen Fellingham and Alison Kerr Miller for their meticulous copyediting and thorough fact checking. Jennifer Thermes's gorgeous map art brought the Vanderbeekers' neighborhood to life, and Karl James Mountford did a magical job with the stunning jacket art.

A giant thank-you to the team at Curtis Brown, in particular the amazing and indomitable Ginger Clark, who deserves eternal wombat happiness, and the wonderful Tess Callero, who deserves frolicking puppies for all her days. There are not enough double chocolate pecan cookies in the world to sufficiently thank Holly Frederick for her relentless belief in me and in this book.

I'm endlessly grateful for my two writing partners who provide daily encouragement and loving company, Sarah Farivar-Hayes and Janice Nimura, kindred spirits in the truest sense. My readers and dear friends deserve so much gratitude, most especially Lauren Hart, Laura Shovan, Katie Graves-Abe, Emily Rabin, and Harrigan Bowman. A very special thanks to Lev Rosen, my mentor and friend, for his punishing (yet encouraging) feedback.

A big hug to Jayme and Anne Brentan, who encouraged me to start this journey in the first place. Lots of gratitude to the Glaser family, with extra love to Michael and Kathleen for their relentless support and encouragement.

I owe so much to the communities that have inspired and supported me, most especially the fine folks at the Town School, Lucy Moses School, Book Riot, the New York Society Library, the Book Cellar, and my Harlem neighborhood. I am incredibly grateful to Nurit Pacht and Monica Stein-Krausz, gifted musicians who pour so much beauty into the world through their music.

Finally, much love to my daughters, Kaela and Lina, who inspire me with their funny antics and joyful spirits, and to Dan, my husband and best friend, who funded hundreds of cups of tea so this story could be written.

KARINA YAN GLASER

THE VANDERBEEKERS
and the HIDDEN GARDEN

Turn the page for a sneak peek of

THE VANDERBEEKERS
and the HIDDEN GARDEN

When catastrophe strikes their beloved upstairs neighbor, the Vanderbeekers must band together to do what they do best: make a plan. They have nineteen days to turn the ivy-ridden, possibly haunted, abandoned lot down the street into the best community garden in Harlem. But creating a garden from scratch is not as easy as it seems, and with no money, absolutely zero gardening experience, and the threat of a slick real estate developer eyeing the land, the Vanderbeekers face their greatest challenge yet.

One

"This is the most boring summer in the whole history of the world," nine-year-old Oliver Vanderbeeker announced. He was wearing basketball shorts and a faded blue T-shirt, and his hair was sticking out in every direction.

"It's only the first week of summer vacation," Miss Josie, the Vanderbeekers' second-floor neighbor, pointed out. The Vanderbeekers, who lived on the ground floor and first floor of a brownstone in Harlem, spent a lot of time on the second floor when their mother was busy baking for her clients. Miss Josie had her hair in curlers and was watering her many trays of seedlings, which covered the dining room table. When she was finished, she stepped over to a window box, clipped a few small purple flowers, and put them in a bud vase before handing it to Laney. "Bring these to Mr. Jeet, won't you, dear?"

Laney, five and a quarter years old and the youngest of Oliver's four sisters, stopped tying ribbons around the ears of her rabbit, Paganini, and stood up. She wore a silver skirt made of sparkly tulle, a purple T-shirt, and sparkly red shoes. The shoes were slippery on the bottom, so she shuffled slowly over to Mr. Jeet, careful not to spill the water in the vase. Paganini hopped close by her heels, shaking his head, causing his ears to flip around and the ribbons to launch in different directions.

"How are you bored already?" Mr. Beiderman asked. Mr. Beiderman was their third-floor neighbor and landlord, and up until half a year ago, he hadn't left his apartment in six years. He had almost refused to renew their lease back in December. But the Vanderbeeker kids had managed to convince him to let them stay, and now they were working on getting him outside the brownstone. He visited the Vanderbeekers as well as Miss Josie and her husband, Mr. Jeet, almost

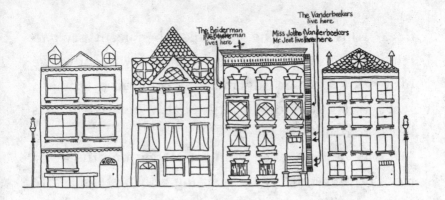

The Beiderman
Mr. Beiderman
lives here

Miss Josie Vanderbeekers
Mr. Jeet live here

The Vanderbeekers
live here

daily, but he had never left the building once in all that time.

Oliver slumped into a sunshine-yellow vinyl chair at the kitchen table, his elbows on the metal tabletop, his hands propping up his head. "There's nothing to do. Nothing I *can* do, anyways."

Oliver watched Miss Josie pull a shoebox down from a high cupboard and lift the top off. Inside were a dozen pill bottles. One by one, she opened bottles and shook pills into a cup. "And what do you want to do?" she asked.

"Text my friends," Oliver said immediately. "Watch basketball videos on YouTube. Play *Minecraft.*"

Mr. Beiderman flattened his mouth into a straight

line. "Kids today," he muttered, then went back to reading out loud to Mr. Jeet. The book was about the history of roses in England. Oliver noticed that Mr. Jeet's eyes fluttered closed, probably because he was bored to death.

Jessie Vanderbeeker, who was a few months away from turning thirteen, was sitting on Miss Josie's fire escape, reading a biography about the famous physicist Chien-Shiung Wu. She leaned her head through the kitchen window between a curtain of ivy tendrils trailing down from Mr. Beiderman's planters above. Her frizzy hair caught onto some of the ivy, making her look electrocuted. "Oliver, seriously," Jessie said. "You're worse than Herman Huxley."

"Herman Huxley!" Oliver spluttered. Being compared to Herman Huxley was like being compared to gum on the bottom of your shoe or jellyfish in a lake on a beautiful summer day when all you wanted to do was cannonball off the dock into the water. Herman Huxley complained about everything, including cold weather, hot weather, and his brand-new Nikes, which any other kid would sell their most prized possessions for.

"Yup," Jessie said, whipping out her new-as-of-last-week phone and punching it with her thumbs.

Oliver felt a wave of pure green jealousy wash over him as Jessie flaunted her phone.

Jessie continued talking, her eyes never leaving the screen. "You know Mama and Papa got this for me so I can keep in touch with Isa." She disappeared back behind the curtain of ivy.

Oliver glared in her direction. It wasn't fair. Isa, yet *another* sister and Jessie's twin, had been chosen for some special three-week-long orchestra camp four hours away by car, but that didn't mean she and Jessie should have whatever they wanted.

Hyacinth, age seven and the sister who annoyed Oliver the least, spoke up from her perch on the arm-rest of Mr. Jeet's chair, where she was working on a new type of knitting using only her fingers—no nee-dles. By wrapping yarn around her fingers and doing some complicated looping, she created a rope of yarn that fell to the ground. "Tell Isa I love her and miss her a million, trillion times. And then put that unicorn emoji at the end, and lots of those pink hearts." Next to her was Franz, her basset hound, who sneezed three times, then nudged Hyacinth's foot with his nose.

"Ha!" said Oliver triumphantly. "She can't even do emojis on that stupid flip phone."

"Language," reminded Miss Josie. She handed Oliver the cup of pills—there were, like, a hundred pills in there!—and a glass of water. "Bring these to Mr. Jeet, will you, dear?"

Oliver unglued himself from his chair and walked to Mr. Jeet. Mr. Jeet wore his customary crisp button-down shirt, a lavender bow tie, and ironed gray slacks. Oliver did not understand why Mr. Jeet *voluntarily* dressed up every day. He was a jeans-and-T-shirt guy himself; the dirtier the clothes, the better the mojo. After he put the pills on the little table by Mr. Jeet's seat, next to a framed photo of the Jeets' twelve-year-old grandnephew Orlando posing with a science fair trophy, he dragged himself back to his chair and slumped into it.

"Why don't you play basketball?" Miss Josie suggested.

"No one's around," he mumbled. "Everyone's at camp. *Basketball* camp."

"Angie isn't at basketball camp," Miss Josie said, referring to his next-door neighbor and friend, who was also the best basketball player in their elementary school.

"She's going to summer school in the mornings. Something about an advanced math extra-credit course." Oliver shuddered.

"I'm sure your mom would love it if you cleaned your room," Miss Josie suggested.

"I cleaned it last month," Oliver said.

"You could read."

"Uncle Arthur forgot to bring books the last time he came to visit."

Miss Josie tsked sympathetically. She knew how much Oliver depended on his monthly book delivery from his uncle, who provided him with every story a kid could wish for.

Mr. Beiderman got up from his chair. "I've got to check on Princess Cutie. Sometimes she scales the curtains and can't get down." Princess Cutie was Mr. Beiderman's cat, which Hyacinth had given him and Laney had named. Mr. Beiderman walked to the door.

"I can teach you how to knit," Hyacinth offered her brother, holding her knitted rope in the air.

"If I ever take up knitting, feel free to stab me in the heart," Oliver replied.

"You can push me and Paganini on the tire swing," Laney suggested, her eyes brightening.

Oliver yawned. "It's too hot."

"Isa would do it," Laney grumbled.

Miss Josie tapped her chin with a finger. "Ooh, I know!"

"You're not going to talk about us making that disgusting piece of land next to the church into a garden again, are you?" Oliver said at the same time Miss Josie exclaimed, "You can make that unused land next to the church into a garden!"

Miss Josie's recommendation was met with collective boos.

"That place is haunted," Laney said. "Isa said so."

Hyacinth nodded. "I don't like walking past it. Isa said the vines that wrap around the gate reach out and grab people when they walk by."

"It's *not* haunted!" Jessie called out. "It has never been scientifically proven that ghosts actually exist."

"How do you know?" Oliver countered. "Have you studied them?"

"Think how nice it would be to have a place to rest in the middle of a hot day," Miss Josie continued. "People could get into the dirt and even plant vegetables! I'm sure Triple J would approve." Triple J was the church's pastor.

"Do you miss working at the botanical garden, Miss Josie?" Jessie asked, pushing aside the ivy so she could look inside. Miss Josie had been an educator at the New York Botanical Garden in the Bronx.

"I do miss it," Miss Josie replied. "I worked there for forty-five years. That's how I met Mr. Jeet. He was a groundskeeper, and he seemed to show up wherever I was. The rest is history." She smiled in Mr. Jeet's direction. Mr. Jeet was letting Hyacinth give him one pill at a time; he was slowly swallowing them with water and grimacing after each one. He sure had to take a lot of pills.

"If you had a garden, you could plant delicious things for Paganini to eat," Miss Josie suggested to Laney.

"Ooh, he would *love* that!" Laney replied. Paganini's ears twitched at the sound of his name; then he jumped into a ceramic pot that held a ficus tree. Miss

Josie gently lifted him out before he kicked dirt all over the floor, then set him on Mr. Jeet's lap.

Mr. Jeet used his right hand (his left hand still had limited mobility after his stroke two years ago) to play with Paganini's ears. His words came out slowly. "You're—lucky—you're—cute." He leaned down while Paganini sat up, and they did a nose bump.

Oliver rested his head on the cool metal table. It felt good against his cheek. "A garden sounds like a lot of work."

"Herman Huxley," Jessie sang from the window. "You are *so* like him."

Oliver was tired of his sister and her stupid comments and her stupid phone. "Stop saying that! You don't know anything!"

"Don't be mean to me because you're jealous of my phone," Jessie shot back, climbing through the window.

"Okay, kids," Miss Josie interjected. "Why don't I put out some tea and cookies—"

But Oliver didn't want tea and cookies. He wanted the last word. "Why do you need a phone, anyways? It's not like you got into science camp and need to stay in contact with Mama and Papa. Isa is probably off having a great time without you, while you're stuck here all summer doing nothing."

"Oliver!" Mr. Jeet called out. Paganini leaped off his lap and onto the carpet, then scurried under an armchair. Mr. Jeet tried to get out of his chair, his face ashen and his arms shaking as he braced himself on the armrests. "Please—Oliver—no—fight—" But before he could finish his sentence, his knees buckled and he fell into Hyacinth.

"Miss Josie, help!" cried Hyacinth, struggling to support Mr. Jeet's weight.

"Jeet!" cried Miss Josie, running toward him.

Mr. Beiderman burst through the door just as Mr. Jeet crumpled to the floor. Hyacinth knocked the medicine cup over as she fell into the side table. The pills fell to the floor and scattered in every direction.